PRAISE FOR
JUST ANOTHER JIHADI JANE

"[Khair] gets behind the flat headlines to the three-dimensional human story and takes its pulse with unflinching honesty. This is a gripping, compassionate and truthful novel, written in prose of unobtrusive beauty."
— **Neel Mukherjee, author of *The Lives of Others*, shortlisted for the Man Booker Prize**

"This powerful, compelling, urgent novel succeeds in being compassionate towards its principal characters without flinching from the full horror of their choices."
—**Amitav Ghosh, author of *Sea of Poppies*, shortlisted for the Man Booker Prize**

"Khair ventures into the space [between rabid Islamophobia and fundamentalist Islamism] with rare courage and truthfulness, in the process also forcing the reader to look both inwards and outwards more carefully and question where we are headed. It is not just a piece of excellent fiction; it is a very necessary and urgent reminder for all of us to examine our own views and prejudices."
—**Rupa Bajua, *The Hindu***

"When you're tired of reading the umpteenth news report on ISIS, you may want to pick up this work of 'fiction,' to allow yourself to confront everything that hard news may not be able to tell you.... Jamilla's plain speaking voice hides deeper, complex truths—some spoken and others left to our imagination—making us question our prejudices and fears all along."
—*The Huffington Post*, **India**

"This thought-provoking book is a tragic, fictional story which might as well be true for many. The book helps to understand the process of brainwashing, the fanaticism and the 'recruitment' through social media employed by fanatics to lure vulnerable people. It also lays bare the horror of being a part of the terror gang. It's heart-wrenching and painful."
—*Hindustan Times*

"In his wise, nuanced evocation of a young British woman's soul-devouring love affair with Islamic State, Tabish Khair powerfully exposes the religious hypocrisy and bloodlust of one of this era's most magnetic and ruthless movements. This novel's triumph—and the world's tragedy—is that Jamilla's haunting, searing experience does not read like a work of fiction. This is not just a writer's nightmare: it is ours."
—**Liz Jensen, author of** *The Ninth Life of Louis Drax*

JUST ANOTHER JIHADI JANE

TABISH KHAIR

Interlink Books

An imprint of Interlink Publishing Group, Inc.
Northampton, Massachusetts

First published 2017 by

INTERLINK BOOKS
An imprint of Interlink Publishing Group, Inc.
46 Crosby Street, Northampton, Massachusetts 01060
www.interlinkbooks.com

Library of Congress Cataloging-in-Publication Data

Names: Khair, Tabish, author.
Title: Just another Jihadi Jane / Tabish Khair.
Description: Northampton, MA : Interlink Books, an imprint of Interlink
   Publishing Group, Inc., [2016]
Identifiers: LCCN 2016034006 | ISBN 9781566560672 (pbk.)
Subjects: LCSH: Political fiction.
Classification: LCC PR9499.3.K427 J87 2016 | DDC 823/.92--dc23
LC record available at https://lccn.loc.gov/2016034006

Printed and bound in the United States of America

To request our complete 48-page catalog, please call us
toll free at 1-800-238-LINK, visit our website at
www.interlinkbooks.com, or write to
Interlink Publishing, 46 Crosby Street, Northampton, MA 01060

Dedicated to the memory of Louie Borges Frost
(1997-2016), who filled the lives of his family—
his parents (my friends), Simon and Sussi, and
his sister, Amanda—and everyone who knew him
with joy and laughter.

TABLE OF CONTENTS

These Vs are all the versuses of life
from LEEDS V. DERBY, Black/White
and (as I've known to my cost) man v. wife,
Communist v. Fascist, Left v. Right,

class v. class as bitter as before,
the unending violence of US and THEM,
personified in 1984
by Coal Board MacGregor and the NUM,

Hindu/Sikh, soul/body, heart v. mind,
East/West, male/female, and the ground
these fixtures are fought on's Man, resigned
to hope from his future what his past never found.

– Tony Harrison, in his poem *v.*

READING SCHEME

Don't ask me for too many details. The devil is in the details, they say. Well, the police are there too, and the antiterror squad. There is death in the details, and there is guilt, crime, and persecution. Details leave scars; they call for vengeance. No, I won't give you too many details. I will give you names of places and people, but seldom the exact ones. Like it or not; make what you can of what I say—for you are a writer, and I will leave this story in your safekeeping. Remember, I am a woman who started off with the conviction that there should be nothing but truth. The One Truth, the Only Truth. I was suckled on that conviction. Ameena wasn't. I felt I had the truth; Ameena was seeking the truth.

Yes, her name is false too.

When did I first meet Ameena? I don't recall. But Ameena told me, in those days in Syria when she could only whisper of the past in a dark room, she told me that it had been in the playground of our school, where she had been sheltering behind the slide, smoking a cigarette. It was a cold grey day, with a hint of rain, a normal day in that part of England. It was a school with a small playground, strewn with litter around the corner, netted from the streets with high wire, and a grubby, grey building with ugly graffiti at the back, also the sort that is normal in that part of England.

"You'd come up to me, you know, and told me that A shouldn't smoke," Ameena said to me, "You were a scarfie, a ninja, no, a nunja; remember A used t'call yer that? All wrapped up, not a strand of hair showing, solemn as always. A'd noticed yer before; yer wor t'most solemn girl in t'class. You never joked with t'boys. But wor always fallin' over to help smaller kids."

"What did you do?" I had asked her, caressing her feverish brow in the dark. We were in a school building then too, in Syria, but it was a very different landscape, a very different education.

"A think A told yer to bugger off," she said, and the memory, the coarse language, so unusual in that place, all of it made her laugh, which caused her to double over in pain from the lacerations on her body.

***

I have no memory of this meeting with Ameena. My earliest memory of her is that of a small girl, with an advanced camera, a Nikon I think, zoom lens and all. She would go about taking street shots. We had no camera in our flat, but Ameena was a dedicated photographer. We must have been twelve or thirteen then. But I remember that by the time we were fifteen, we were friends. In my recollection, this happened because Ameena and her mum moved into our building, the building where my father had a flat.

Do I need to describe the building? You know the streets, where buildings grow straight from the footpath, one after another, their façades bland, with blank windows staring like the eyes of a zombie. You press a buzzer to be allowed in. If the buzzer is working. There are newspapers and wrappers strewn in the foyer and under the staircase. Sometimes the buildings have a lift. Our building had one.

It smelled of sweat and deodorant. "Max capacity three," a notice said.

You think that sounds bad? It was much worse when I was a child. The lift would smell of vomit and beer then. And there were used condoms and syringes lying about. Then, of course, more of us moved in and more of them moved out. Some were glad to leave; some gave us the finger. But they left, slowly, one by one, the so-called white working class. Or the white drinking class. The so-called brown working class moved in. It was not the brown drinking class though; it was mostly the Muslim working class. The smell of vomit and beer disappeared. The syringes and condoms disappeared. The graffiti got multilingual. All the rest stayed as it was.

My father had a two-bedroom flat there, with a small study that had been my bedroom as long as I could recall. When I was ten or eleven, he had a heart attack. My brother, Mohammad, who was eighteen then, hustled himself out of school, took a driving test and started running Abba's cab for the time being. Abba stayed home, reading the Quran, and getting even more bitter about the world. He was going to get back to work, but never really did. Mohammad was bringing in more money than Abba ever did. Occasionally, Abba would take one of Mohammad's shifts, but mostly he stayed home, complaining. Often he went to the mosque. He had always gone to the mosque on Fridays, Mohammad in tow. He never took me, though some of his friends would let their daughters tag along. But not Abba. It is against our religion, he said. Women have to pray separately from men.

He insisted, however, that Mohammad and I attend classes in conversational Arabic—which, I suppose you know, is almost another language from the Arabic of the Quran—that the mosque also offered, in a side room. We are *Syeds*; my father considered Arabic his mother tongue, even though he only knew Quranic Arabic. I guess no one had spoken Arabic in our family for centuries! But Abba took pride in returning us to conversational Arabic. I took pride in it, too, for his sake, much more than Mohammad, who never picked up more than the fundamentals, while I supplemented the side-room classes with correspondence courses. Perhaps I wanted to impress Abba, to be taken to the mosque as Mohammad was, dressed in clean clothes, standing by Abba's side. It never happened; I learned to go to the mosque's prayer hall only with other women and girls.

I grew up accepting such judgements from my father—and from other men. Sometimes women too, of course, but my mother never seemed to have a real opinion. She was a timid woman—I assume she is still alive—who had been lovingly browbeaten by her father, and then her husband, and then this incomprehensible new country. In due course, she would be lovingly browbeaten by her son too. But I am anticipating matters.

***

Ameena had a very different background. Both of us spoke Urdu at home, but Ameena's mum was a working woman. Her parents had grown up in Bangalore; they had married in India before moving to England, where her dad was posted by some multinational and then switched jobs to settle down—because he liked it so much here, Ameena once said, and she did ironic things with her eyes and eyebrows. All this was ancient history; it happened long before we met.

I guess Ameena wouldn't have moved into our neighbour-hood if her parents had not divorced. They had divorced years ago; Ameena told me that she was seven or eight when they separated.

Her father was a banker, I think; anyway, something in the financial world—something that fetched good money, and required flashy cars and custom-made suits. He walked and talked briskly. To me, he looked like an older version of that Indian tennis player, what's his name—Leander Paes. I met Ameena's dad only a few times, when he came to collect or deliver Ameena at our building or in school, and, once, to help her move. I used to be tenser on such occasions than Ameena. Though he, Ameena's father, was always charming and gracious. I have to concede that. He had his wife or partner with him on at least two occasions. She stayed in the car, texting on her iPhone. A white woman, with limp, thin blonde hair. I hated her then, because Ameena hated her. "This is his number three," she hissed to me the first time. "He lives with three women?" I whispered back, shocked. "No, this is the third woman he has picked up since leaving my mum," she replied. "He left my mum for one of them," she added. But I didn't need to be told. I had been suckled on the prejudice that good-looking, successful coloured men, unless religious, always left their good, lawful wives for "one of them."

I knew what she meant by "one of them." In those days, Ameena was still smoking on the sly and necking with the boys behind the school building, if she liked a boy or just felt angry at her mum. She particularly liked Alex. Everyone liked Alex. Alex looked like a young David Beckham. He combed his hair like Beckham. He even played soccer like

Beckham. Like Beckham used to, that is. Ameena was in love with Alex. Half the girls in his class, and two classes up and below, were in love with Alex. And Alex, well, Alex was like the mum in that poem by Wendy Cope: he liked them all. Do you know the poem? "Reading Scheme." No? I will tell you about it. It has a role to play in my story.

But when Ameena said "one of them," she did not mean all the Pakistani, Polish, Lebanese, Bangladeshi, Welsh, hybrid, or whatever girls who had a crush on Alex. She meant blonde white girls who dressed in ways that Ameena's mum would not permit her to adopt, and who went about with an aura that said, as big as a billboard in neon, with ping-ping flashing lights, I KNOW ALL ABOUT SEX. Girls who were Lady Gaga on steroids.

Ameena had lovely eyes, liquid and soft, much darker than mine, with the shadow of some unnamed hurt lurking in them. Like a lake at dusk. But you would not call Ameena pretty. You would not call her ugly either. She was a plain-looking girl, with beautiful eyes and thick hair; neither tall nor short, neither shy nor vivacious. She had very little chance with someone like Alex, who did feel her up now and then, I guess out of sheer curiosity. He was always far more interested in me. Most men are. Even today, after all that has happened, I keep this scarf wrapped around my hair because of men's interest in me. It is not because of faith anymore; I still believe in Allah, don't get me wrong, but I do not think Allah is a fashion designer. He observes people's hearts, not their clothes. This is not what Abba believed; this is not what my big brother, Mohammad, believes. This is also not what I believed in those days, when I tried not just to get Ameena to quit smoking, but also to start veiling herself. But now, well, I still keep the scarf on and I still wear loose clothes to avoid male glances. And, honestly, because it makes me feel comfortable in my skin; anything else would be like wearing a spacesuit, given my upbringing. It doesn't help too much, though. I get looked up and down in any case. Even you observed me on the sly. No, don't get flustered. There is probably nothing wrong in noticing a woman. Who knows? I guess it depends on what is in the man's heart. I did not point this out to accuse you; I just wanted you to know that I know. I know that men notice me.

Alex noticed me too. Perhaps even more so because I was part of the small group of girls who observed Islamic precepts or, in any case, what our parents thought were Islamic precepts. Ameena was not one of us, though in those days I was always trying to spread the word. Mohammad had started bringing in pamphlets from some proselytising organisation that he had joined, and I would read them line by line. Later on, I even joined a women's branch of his organisation and spent many evenings calling up people—we were given random numbers—and asking them if I could tell them about the Quran and our prophet, pleeease. It was all about spreading the word—*da'wah* work, we called it. It was the only thing Allah asked of us: to do our duty, live in the right way, and spread the word, the invitation of Islam. I believed in it.

But I was not naïve. I have never been, in such matters. I knew that Alex had the hots for me. The fact that I was so "out of bounds," as James once put it, must have been a strong aphrodisiac for Alex. That and the fact, as our history teacher, a hairless slimy old geezer in his fifties, had lisped in class just the previous year: "I suppose

Jamie here, Jamie would be our idea of Cleopatra, wouldn't she, if she did not mostly hide herself from view." (I hated being called Jamie—my name is Jamilla—but evidently Europeans cannot stop themselves from giving new names to people and places. I guess it must be hard to stop after all those centuries when they went about renaming stuff in the colonies.) In that year—we were fifteen or so, Ameena was already living with her mum in our building, and hence we were commuting together and sometimes hanging out in the school canteen—Alex took to joining us whenever he did not have his short-skirted, fashionable girls around him.

Ameena shone with happiness on these occasions. Alex was always gallant; he flirted with her and paid attention to her. I knew that he was humouring her. In the way he sat himself down at our table, the way he angled his face, so that he could stare at me while seeming to be speaking to Ameena, it was obvious to anyone. But not to Ameena. The girl was gone on Alex: she even referred to him, only when with me of course, as Mr. Ooh la la! It was an expression, pronounced with an American lilt, that Ameena loved. I was dry and short with Alex, but that did not seem to discourage him. I guess he thought it was just some kind of mating game, a complex one, which we, Arabs, Pakis, Iranis, whatever he thought I was, played in our mysterious, intricate lands, but one that would finally end in yet another victory for him.

***

Ameena was still a smoker. But the months we had spent together had made her a more careful dresser. She was no longer wearing the tight jeans and T-shirts, bearing moronic slogans, that she had preferred. Now she was wearing baggies and shirts. No scarf yet, though. And of course not the full hijab that I donned outside school; she still teasingly called me a "nunja."

I had started taking her to the discussion group in the mosque—an all-women one—that I had been attending for a couple of years already. Her mum—I will call her Aunty, which is how I addressed her—did not like this. She was a short, birdlike woman of indeterminate age and almost cropped hair. Mohammad and Abba had commented on that. The almost cropped hair, that is. Also, on the fact that Aunty wore no hijab, not even a scarf, and on occasion went out in trousers and a shirt. Ammi, my mother, had tut-tut-tut-ed and then added, "But, poor woman, she has to work in this country." Abba had growled at Ammi, "Don't be foolish. Is that an excuse to give up on your faith? Do Mohammad and I drink because we have to work in this country? These convent-educated *Indian* Muslims!" Mohammad had laughed the superior laugh that he employed whenever matters of someone's deficiency of faith or his superiority in it were highlighted. Ammi had taken shelter, as she always did, in either the dingy kitchen or her copy of the Quran.

So, no, Ameena's mum, Aunty to me, was not happy about Ameena going to my mosque sessions. But she did not object. I think she was relieved to find Ameena doing something that seemed less dangerous than her fears for her daughter. Aunty and Ameena could seldom talk for long without getting into arguments. Ameena blamed her father for leaving her mum, but, on the few occasions I saw her with her debonair dad, both seemed happy and the best of friends. When Ameena looked at her dad, you could see the adoration in her eyes. Her dad seemed to have little time for Ameena, and behind his back she would be caustic about him and his "number three." But all of it disappeared the moment he appeared, always looking younger and more dapper than the other dads. You would say, maybe, it was only those seconds of meeting and parting that I witnessed. Surely they would have had arguments in between? I doubt it. I have seen divorced kids with their parents: a meeting starts well and ends badly; a meeting starts badly and ends well. But I never saw any sign of unease or any kind of upset between Ameena and her dad when they were together.

With her mum—who toiled hard as a teacher in some school somewhere, and often brought work home—it was different. Ameena was out to irritate her, even run her down. Aunty was not an easy person, or so it appeared to me in those days. She appeared opinionated and nagging. A tooter, she would have been dubbed in school. She was either in a rush or tired, which made her complaining, inattentive, or irritable. Her flat was messier than our flat, with books, magazines, and plates scattered everywhere. I sided with Ameena in all her conflicts with Aunty, even when Ameena was clearly in the wrong. I could see why Ameena's dad had left her mum. Looking back, I am less sure: I now realise I was unconsciously comparing Ameena's mum to my own Ammi, a woman who spoke no English, stayed home, got anxious about the smallest of things, like shopping on her own, never contradicted either Abba or Mohammad, and almost never scolded me for any oversight, real or imagined.

I know Aunty knew about Ameena's smoking; she must have been told about the pranks Ameena had been involved in—this was before we became friends. She would hang out with any boy who gave her some attention, and half the time it would result in some school prank or class warning. The boy—usually a potential dropout—would do something idiotic, and Ameena would wade into it with wide-open eyes. I do not recall where they had lived earlier on—growing financial pressure after her divorce had made Aunty sell her flat and buy something much smaller—but, from the little that Ameena revealed, it was clear that she used to go about with the dregs of her previous neighbourhood. Our school did not have knife-wielding gangs, but in town there were semicriminal youth gangs—Elm Street Gangsters, Knuckledusters, E7th Rydaz—and some boys and girls boasted of hanging out with them after school. Ameena once suggested she used to "know some cool guys" from a "real gang" in her old neighbourhood. No wonder, despite her dated bob-cut, Western trousers, and copies of the *New Statesman*, Aunty did not object when Ameena started fraternising with me and the local mosque crowd.

***

At fifteen (or was she sixteen then?), Ameena was no longer a virgin. In that, she was like "one of them." She did not believe I had never been to bed with a man. Clearly, Alex did not believe it either. Not that it was discussed when Alex was around; it was just in the air. Alex knew Ameena was available; he knew I wasn't. But, as I said, he believed I would be. I guess he believed everyone would be available sooner or later. Available to him, that is.

He had started sitting in our corner during literature class. He would try and position himself in such a manner as to have me between him and Ameena, so that when he turned and said flirtatious things to Ameena, they would need to go through me. The Ice Queen, he used to call me.

The literature teacher was an Indian woman called Mrs. Chatterji—we never found out what her first name was—and she loved English and English poetry with the sort of fanaticism that only the ex-colonised bring to either. She tried to inculcate her love for both in us. This was difficult—she spoke English that was correct and chipped but far from what we spoke, far, to be honest, from what I am employing for your benefit. As for poetry, have you ever tried to teach poetry to fifteen-year-olds?

But Mrs. Chatterji struggled. She devised new ways to get us interested in old poets. I did not realise it then, but she was a resourceful educator: she got us to write limericks on our teachers, she invited performance poets to read in class, she initiated debates and projects on literary issues—including one that I will have to tell you about later on, for it came back to me in a very different phase of my life. That year, she found another way to get us somewhat interested in poetry: she asked us to bring a poem each, per week, to class. Then we had to sit in groups of three or four, exchange the poems and tell each other why we had chosen that particular poem. This worked, at least to the extent that the boys could bring funny limericks and hip hop lyrics, and the girls could download Beyoncé and mushy romantic poems from the Internet. Alex would come up with better poems. He was not an unintelligent boy. His poems would be what you, as a writer yourself, might call poems, I guess. You know, stuff with some awareness of metre and rhyme; stuff that broke poetic convention not out of sheer ignorance but from necessity. I am quoting Mrs. Chatterji. And that is how Wendy Cope's "Reading Scheme" entered my life. Because, you see, every poem that Alex brought had to do with sex; not in any obvious way, or Mrs. Chatterji would have censored it, but clearly enough for him to gaze into my eyes in a significant manner while reciting the lines out to Ameena or whoever else would be in our group. And given Ameena's fascination with the guy, it was impossible for me to manoeuvre her into some other group.

Do you recall "Reading Scheme"? It is a funny poem. But, then, it would be; it is by Wendy Cope. I remember Mrs. Chatterji was particularly glad about this selection by Alex. She would hop around—she was a short, rotund woman, with a pink face and marble eyes—from group to group, inspecting, encouraging, commenting. I used to find her ludicrous. I don't know why, now. I mean, she was fanatical about her poetry, but then I was fanatical about my religion, as were my Abba and Mohammad and all my mosque friends. How could I see the fanaticism in her absolute love for Wordsworth, Byron, Shelley—she was an extreme believer in her Romantic notion of poetry, in the same way as Wahhabis are extremist believers in their notion of Islam—and find it ludicrous, but take my own fanaticism so seriously, so unconditionally?

Anyway, Mrs. Chatterji was delighted with "Reading Scheme"; she usually tried hard to hide her lack of enthusiasm for any verse by a poet who had not been dead and buried for about a century. She asked Alex to read it out aloud. Alex obliged, reciting in his deep voice, looking me in the eye when the suggestive lines came up: "Come, milkman, come!" Quick stare. "The milkman likes Mummy. She likes them all." Stare with a smile. "Here are the curtains. They shut out the sun." Stare with raised eyebrow. "Look at the dog! See him run!" Stare with a slight leer, the stress on "dog."

See, I still remember the lines.

Neither Mrs. Chatterji nor Ameena were noticing the target of Alex's stares. Mrs. Chatterji was fixated on the poem and Ameena on the reciter. Maybe it was this, or maybe it was Alex's impudence. In any case, I reacted strongly to the poem. It is a dexterous poem, using a reading scheme to talk humorously about a suburban mum having an affair with the milkman and being discovered by the husband, all of it narrated through the perspective of her two small children. We had read more adult stuff in literature and history. Usually, though I felt offended by them, I would ignore such texts. But that day I could not. So, when Mrs. Chatterji asked us, as was her custom, to say what we thought of the poem, I blurted out, surprising myself, "Poofy words!"

Mrs. Chatterji did not understand my criticism. Maybe she didn't even fully understand "poofy"; she had grown up in India and spoke a clipped, literary English, like they do on BBC. She started talking about the deftness of the poem and how it is a villanelle, which critics say cannot be used to narrate a story: remember Dylan Thomas's "Do Not Go Gentle into that Good Night," with its beautiful repetitions, its lack of linear progress in terms of action or story? But, look, Wendy Cope has with such cleverness, such dexterity, ah, used the villanelle form to tell us a story, shall we say, an action-story that moves from one point to another in a linear fashion and makes us laugh at the same time. Alex tried to look into my eyes with his knowing smile.

It provoked me further. "Maybe 'tis funny to you," I said, breaking into dialect despite my rigorous attempt (unlike Ameena, especially in those days) to speak "proper" English. "I'll say 'tis an obscene poem, 'tis 'bout a sin me God forbids. 'Bout 'dultery. Raight? That's nowt to use for cheap laughter." Mrs. Chatterji was a bit taken aback by that, but she insisted that it was not an obscene poem; after all, it does not celebrate adultery, does it? The milkman is chased from the bedroom by the gun-toting dad. Couldn't I see the humour, the irony.... "The irony?" I argued back, righteously. Alex looked on with a knowing smile. Finally, Mrs. Chatterji said, "Jamilla, why don't you take this poem home and look at it again? Write 250 words on it, and we will discuss it in class next week. Write whatever you feel about it, but write it down. That is all I want you to do. Think over the poem again and write down what you feel about it."

"But A've told yer: A think nowt of it," I retorted, sticking to the dialect in defiance of Mrs. Chatterji, though she had never tried to get even Ameena to talk "properly."

"That is fine. But just write it down in that case. I will accept whatever you say, as long as you look at the poem again and write down your own views."

Was she trying to get out of the debate, or did she hope that writing down my views would somehow make me relent or take a more nuanced view of the poem? It didn't.

***

I must have spent more time on that 250-word essay than I ever did on any other homework. I was angrier than I had ever been. And, strangely, even then I felt that my anger was in excess of the occasion: I could see that it was a comic poem about a stereotypical escapade; I could admire—for I did remember the Dylan villanelle—Cope's technical dexterity; and I could even feel a smile, the ghost of a smile, forming at some of the lines, especially the refrain of "Look at the dog! See him run," which starts off as a description of the family dog and ends up as a description of the milkman being chased away by the dad and husband. But partly because of that ghostly smile and partly because of Alex's smug confidence, finally, because of Ameena, who claimed to know all about these matters, having done "it" with at least two boys, because of all these factors, and maybe others, the more I felt that my anger was in excess of the occasion, the angrier I got. If I thought, as I did then, that Cope's poem was a dirty little ditch, then what I poured into it was an ocean of pure vehemence, anger that seemed to come from beyond me, and left me feeling angrier.

My essay was full of this pervasive anger. And it was full of quotations from the Quran, the hadith, and even one from the Bible. All about adultery, of course, and sin, chastisement, depravity, divine vengeance. I think the one from the Bible ran something like this: "Do you not know that the unrighteous will not inherit the kingdom of God? Do not be deceived; neither fornicators, nor idolaters, nor adulterers, nor the effeminate, nor homosexuals." I had written more than 250 words; I had written closer to 500, and the gist of it was simple: "Reading Scheme" was a depraved poem about adultery, and in this it reflected the depravity of the West, which had long gone against the will of God, not just as expressed in that most correct of all revelations, the Quran, but also as expressed in their own truncated and much edited version of God's revelations, the Bible.

For this, I warned with quotations from the Quran in the last two paragraphs, much punishment was in store for the West, that den of adultery, fornication, and duplicity, and the sword of the Lord was going to descend on it and all unbelievers everywhere, any moment now.

***

Mrs. Chatterji was in a good mood the next week. She was usually a happy woman, with cheeks that dimpled easily and eyes that would brim with tears when reading a particularly tragic passage in Dickens or Wordsworth, and that day she was in an unusually good mood. She came up to me, and said gaily, "Did you write that essay, Jamilla?" She was one of the few teachers who used my full name. I handed her my essay, grim-faced.

She hopped and skipped back to her desk. She introduced the Wendy Cope poem and our discussion from last week in a few words. Then she read out the poem for the entire class. Finally, still not prepared for the depth of my anger, she started reading out my essay. Her voice faltered in the second paragraph. She stuttered in the third and fourth paragraphs. She fell silent, without noticing it, in the fifth paragraph. She never managed to read out the last few paragraphs. But as her eyes moved down the pages, her face grew paler, and at the end the papers almost slipped out of her hands. I believe she had to steady herself by leaning with an arm on her desk. Then, she said to me, "But, Jamilla, I don't think you get the poem; it is not about morality or God, it is, it is about …" She could not say what it was about. She repeated, weakly, "I don't think you get it."

Alex had been looking at me with a slight smile on his

exquisitely carved lips. All along, he had been looking at me as if my reaction to the poem was a personal matter between him and me, a lover's tiff rather than an intellectual issue. Now he drawled, raising any eyebrow, "No, Jamie Baby, the problem is that you just don't get it." More than the lazy "Jamie Baby," it was the knowing way in which he stressed "it" that made me reach over and slap him, hard, on the face.

***

You can imagine the rest. Alex was lightly reprimanded by Mrs. Chatterji; I was sent to the Head for a talk. The Head read my essay and decided to have a talk with my parents instead. He wrote me a letter to give my parents and said he would call them if they did not contact him within a week. He need not have bothered. I was not the kind of person who hid things from her family. I told my parents, who told Mohammad to go and talk to the Head—and Mohammad basically gave the Head and Mrs. Chatterji a more emphatic rendition of my position on the matter. Not having read the poem, and having no time for poetry—after all, as I was also brought up believing, why read a poem when the Quran contains *divine* poetry?—he had little time for the Head's and Mrs. Chatterji's points, and instead attempted to cow them into silence by claiming that they were attacking our religious beliefs. He called for a blanket ban on such poems in school. I think there was a row of some sort, and the Head threatened to take it up elsewhere, while Mrs. Chatterji pleaded for it to be simply forgotten, and Mohammad thumped them with the Quran and the Bible—he was good at quoting both. I guess it might all have escalated if, the very next day, my father had not had a second heart attack.

There were about two weeks between my slapping Alex, Mohammad's visit to the Head, and my father's second heart attack. I did not get to talk to Ameena in those days. She had taken Alex's side. I saw her in the school, always hanging on Alex's arms, looking radiant. They were an item now, said the girls. They sat together in class. He had inserted her into his group, the sporty boys with slicked hair, the girls who dressed, laughed, and walked like models. She was a duckling in that herd of swans. But she was happy, I guess. Alex had eyes in class only for her.

I thought I knew what Alex was playing at. I would have tried to warn Ameena, but she avoided me. She even went home with Alex, and she met him in the mornings outside school. They met for walks in our neighbourhood park. On the few occasions our paths crossed, she avoided my gaze, but Alex looked at me and smiled. He had a charming smile.

One day after school I caught him posing elaborately for Ameena and her camera in the park. I could not help quipping to Ameena, my eyebrows arched, as I went past them: "Ah, you are into portraits now." To which she replied, "Everyone evolves"; and Alex added, with his pure, innocent laugh: "Except some, we know."

Despite this, once I went to her flat. But Aunty told me Ameena was out; the awkward way she said it made it clear that Ameena was home and avoiding me. I did not go back. And then my father had his second heart attack.

This time he lasted only three days, in the intensive care unit of a hospital. They were doing everything possible, the doctors told Mohammad and my Ammi, who had to be forced to leave the hospital every time we visited him. She could not understand why the doctors would not allow her to sleep in my father's room. "I can sleep on a sheet on the floor, tell them that, just tell them that," she begged Mohammad and me. Of course, we couldn't; we knew it would not be permitted. Once she found a Bangladeshi doctor and trailed after him, pleading in Urdu, until he escaped behind closed doors.

Then my father was gone. Just like that—an entire life, at least two different countries, so much hope, so much despair, so many words, so much silence … all gone. The emptiness he left behind grew larger each day, especially after the funeral, and then, slowly, without me realising it, it started filling up, like a hole in the dry sand fills up, almost imperceptibly, with unnoticed sliding grains of sand.

Mohammad took care of the burial. Some of my father's friends and some of Mohammad's came over for the function in our house and the mosque. Ammi and I were not allowed to go to the burial—we were women. We had not expected to go. But Ammi wanted to visit his grave later on, and pro-tested, weakly—the only time I remember her protesting at all—when Mohammad and his bearded friends told her that she shouldn't. "But we used to be allowed to go to graveyards back home," she said. It was all wrong, she was told. These practices have to stop. Women should not go to graveyards. It was all wrong in the past, not the true Islamic path. They took turns quoting various texts to her. They told her that women are too weak to be allowed into a graveyard. Such soft and emotional hearts they have, for they are wives and mothers. They said that women weep on graves, and open lamentation over the departed is contrary to Islamic beliefs.

My mother did not protest much. She had listened to my father all her life; she listened to Mohammad now. She did what she had always done on such occasions: she took to her well-thumbed copy of the Quran, reading it over and over again, slowly, painstakingly, and as always her face lost its harried look when she read the holy book, she even seemed to me at times to have grown younger, as if a small girl, hidden in her wizened body, wrapped up in her folds of cloth, was suddenly peeping out of her eyes.

You ask, what about me? Did I want to visit my father's grave?

There was nothing to prevent me. I could have gone without telling anyone. It was not illegal in England, of course, and no guardian of the graveyard would have stopped me. But remember how I was then: I had deep faith in my religion. I still have faith. But in those days, it was the religion that had come to me through Abba. I was loyal to my religion because I was loyal to my father, who had suffered much to give us a decent life.

Not suffered in the material sense, though that might have happened too: who knows how he raised the money to buy his cab, who knows what hoodlums might not have accosted him, what drunks not urinated in his bloody Paki cab? My mother often recalled the time—this was before Mohammad was born, sometime in the early 90s or late 80s, when Abba had a swastika spray-painted on his cab one night, its windows smashed, and they had trouble getting insurance to cover the repairs, so she had to sell some of her jewellery to raise the money. But Abba merely suggested such trials; he never dwelled on them, accepting them as part and parcel of his working life. What he dwelled on, relentlessly, ceaselessly, obsessively, were his spiritual sufferings: how he was lost in this den of iniquity and vices, this realm of the unbelievers, how he feared that his lineage would be sucked into the morass and vileness of the West and disappear not just from the land of his origin, which was inevitable, but also from the benevolent sight of Allah. His father, my grandfather that is, had left a town called Phansa somewhere in India to move to Pakistan during the Partition, losing a sister to communal violence *en route*. Look at me, my father would say, and his friends—who often had similar trajectories—would shake their heads in agreement: "Look at me. My dear respected father left the realm of unbelievers for the nation of the pure, and I had to leave that land for this island of impurity." Mohammad and I had grown up with that burden, and I had the example of my mother—trusting unquestioningly in the men around her—to cement my faith. What choice did I have?

No, I did not even think of visiting my father's grave. You see, above all, I wanted to stay faithful to *his* Islam.

***

The matter of my critique of the Cope poem had been quietly forgotten by the time I returned to school after an absence of about a week. The Head called me into his room to offer me his condolences. Mrs. Chatterji, tears in her eyes, gave me a beautiful edition of Kahlil Gibran's *The Prophet*, which I received with ill grace, as I took it as implicit criticism of my faith, but which, looking back, I assume was the closest she could get to understanding my version of Islam; the book had been offered to me as a gesture of love.

So wrapped up was I in my own loss that it took me a couple of days, or maybe more, to notice that Ameena sat alone now. She was not with Alex or his group. Alex was seeing another girl, from a different class, I was informed when I asked. Hadn't I seen her? She was this elegant ballet dancer and netball player. What about Ameena? The girls laughed. Easy come, easy go, they said. Ameena had lost the few friends she had in the past; she had ignored them in the weeks when she was part of the flashy crowd, hanging on Alex's arm. Now they were cold to her. And, of course, she had ceased to exist for Alex's crowd.

She sat alone in the canteen. Sometimes James joined her. Have I told you about James? I haven't? James was one of those boys you find in every class. His body seemed to be slightly beyond his control. He was always bumping into things. No sportsman, of course, but unlike the other nerds in class, he liked to play sports. He had mousey hair and a startlingly pink face. No girl ever fell for him, but he was always falling in love with the most beautiful girls in school. He would write them poems—innocent little ones about the heart's devotion and the meeting of minds—for a semester or two, and then, faced with disdain or impassivity, he would fall in love with another beautiful girl. If he had fallen in love with someone like Ameena, he might have had a chance—but James was one of those men who seem to choose women who are bound to reject them, almost as if they are frightened, deep down in their hearts, of being accepted.

So, when James joined Ameena, it was not because he was in love with her. He was not writing her poems, by any means. When James started writing a girl poems, the entire class knew, because he would pass the poem to the girl in front of others, telling her: this, ahem, is for you, ahem. There was nothing underhanded about James. I guess that is why he was not bullied or scoffed as some of the other nerds were. He went about his own life, strange as it was, with a kind of openness and generosity that I saw then but came to appreciate fully only much later. He was also the only boy in class who would discuss serious matters with you—like your faith or God—without joshing your ideas as the sporty crowd did, or patronising you in a superior way as the stiffs did. So when James joined Ameena, he did so because that was how he was—he noticed what was being done to Ameena and he did not want to be part of it.

It was James who filled me in about what had happened. Not that I could not have imagined it. It was the usual stuff. Alex had tired of Ameena and indicated it to her in his usual way—Alex was not a boor and, I guess, he did not want to be unkind. But Ameena did not or could not see the signs. She hung on to Alex and his crowd, making herself ludicrous and pathetic at times. This went on for a week or so, until Alex could not take it anymore—he had another girlfriend by then, the ballet dancer from a senior year—and one day he told Ameena in public to "fuck off." His crowd laughed at her. That was the end of their relationship. Alex had not wanted anything other than that. He just wanted to be rid of this embarrassing ex-lover. But, being who he was, he neither realised nor really cared that his public rebuff would also mean the end of Ameena in school.

***

Ameena sat alone, and usually turned away from me if I was nearby, as if she wanted to avoid seeing me. If the others did not make space for her in their groups, unless they had to under a teacher's supervision, Ameena studiously ignored them too. James was the only person she made space for.

I did not approach her because of that. Or perhaps I was still resentful about her taking Alex's side. In any case, it was James who asked me, one day at lunch, why I did not speak to Ameena. "You are not like the others," he said, "Why've yer blanked her too? That's nasteh." I denied that I had blanked her. "She doesn't want me to speak to her," I replied. "Have yer given it a shot?" he asked in his nonargumentative manner. I was quiet.

The next day, during a break, I went up to the playground slide; Ameena usually smoked behind it. I did not know what I would say to her, but I could not ignore the pricking of conscience that James's words had induced. Ameena was there. But she was not smoking a cigarette. She was smoking a vapour pen.

"Vaping for fun or quitting?" I joked, awkwardly.

"Trying," she replied.

I nodded.

"We have missed you at the mosque," I said to her, after an awkward pause.

"Off me beaten path," she retorted, with a sarcastic laugh. Then she relented. "Well, missed y'all too," she added, puffing and looking away.

"Maybe I can knock when I go there next?"

"Save me soul, eh?" She looked away, and then, just when I thought I had been brusquely dismissed, she added, "Maybe yer can knock."

***

That is how Ameena came to be a regular of my mosque group, which was, around then, being taken over by "sisters and brothers" from Hizb ut-Tahrir, who had no patience with "Western deviance." She started borrowing and then buying books about Islam. I guided her. I was happy to guide her. I had been told that every person you bring to the faith—or bring back to the faith—opens a new gate of heaven for you.

I can see you looking curiously at me; you are wondering if that is what "radicalised" her, as the media like to put it. Mutual support, group grievance, slippery slope: I can see all these easy terms popping up in your head. But, really, what radicalised Ameena? Was it the religion she learnt in the mosque? I concede that the group I was with had probably the strictest interpretation of Islam among the many Muslims who used our mosque; so, in a way, I radicalised Ameena. I thought so for months, when I finally started thinking about such matters, and I blamed myself terribly, especially after what happened to Ameena. I still do not shrug away my role in all of it, but I ask you, are you sure it was the mosque that radicalised Ameena? Why Ameena out of a thousand or more? Was it only the mosque? Was it only me, and my father's and brother's Islam? Or was it also Ameena's parents' divorce? Was it that ghostly hurt and anger lurking in Ameena's lucid eyes? Was it her lost love for Alex? Was it the way her friends snubbed her? Was it her mother's strong disapproval of the Islamic scarf?

Because, after quitting smoking, Ameena took to tying her hair with a scarf, tightly, the way I and some other Muslim girls did. Unlike me, she did not put on a niqab outside home or school (I had just graduated from the hijab to the face-covering niqab), but she started using a scarf and wearing loose, nondescript clothes. Slacks instead of jeans; long-sleeve shirts instead of jerseys. Her mum did not like it. The scarves, that is. They argued. They always had. But in the past, Aunty was worried about Ameena's smoking and the boys she hung around with; now she was worried about her religion and the girls she went about with. She could not express her worry in public, at least around us. After all, she was a Muslim, and how could a Muslim prevent another Muslim from following what she thought was her religion? Perhaps because she could not openly stop Ameena from going out with me or going to the mosque or tying a scarf or wearing baggy clothes, Aunty pestered and harangued her even more behind doors. Ameena would relate their fights to me with a degree of relish. In the past, deep down, Ameena must have felt that her mum was morally justified when she tried to stop her from smoking or sleeping around. But now Ameena knew that she had the moral upper hand.

What about Ameena's father? Did he notice? Did he object? I don't know: I suspect that Ameena and her father had adopted fixed roles in an elaborate game of convenience and resentment. They behaved differently when they were together; they saw only what they wished to see, especially Ameena's father. It was convenient for him, as was the resentment that Ameena harboured for Aunty. Moreover, I wonder if Ameena's father, despite his Western ways, his tennis star looks, did not feel that Ameena was safer growing into adulthood with a scarf around her head than in a miniskirt?

MY BROTHER'S WEDDING

Over the next few years, Ameena and I became the best of mates. We hardly did anything without the other. We did our homework and watched TV together; we went shopping together; we went to the mosque together; we surfed together for Islamic preaching on YouTube.

She liked spending time at our place. You have to realise that I was not the kind of girl who hung around in malls or went to McDonald's. No pop concerts, not just any film in the theatres, no raves. There were not that many places for a girl like me. Once in a while, we visited a like-minded friend or saw a "safe" movie, sometimes we went to a lecture or to the library, and we met with our discussion and social welfare group at the mosque. There were several of them, and I belonged to an all-girls group, under the tutelage of a middle-aged woman. We were the ones who wrapped ourselves up most severely, the ones who never allowed a frivolous smile on our faces. For a while, Ameena, who still dressed more casually than us despite her scarf, stuck out in the group. But no one said anything to her, I am sure. And she had stopped calling me a nunja by then! But all this still left us with lots of time: our group met only for definite occasions. The rest of the time, we had to meet at home.

Ameena's flat was difficult for us, mostly because we were certain Aunty would object to some of the preachers and speakers we followed on Facebook and YouTube.

These were people who either preached a very strict version of Islam or highlighted the hypocrisies of the West: the political double standards, the arms industry, the orange-clothed prisoners in places like Guantanamo, the lack of international democracy, the inability of the West to hold Israel responsible for human rights violations, the role of oil money in the conflicts of the Middle East. Aunty might not have objected to the latter kind, for much of what they said was not unusual from the leftist perspective—except that the ideologues we listened to had a religious explanation for everything. Economics was just a subtext; finally, they argued or suggested, this was an attack on Islam, and it had been going on from the time of the first crusades. Look at the way the Christians have been circling and hemming in the Muslim world, they proclaimed. Look at the wildly sprouting military bases: did any Muslim nation have a single military base in a Christian country? No wonder, they scoffed, Bush II slipped and used words like "crusade"—before his damage controllers stepped in to assuage the consciences of those duplicitous leftists of the West, who did not even have the guts to face up to the truth of the matter and instead quoted that ex-Jew, Marx.

Such YouTube films could be watched in my flat. My Ammi, it is true, almost never watched them, but Mohammad would, if he was around and not resting. He would comment on the commentary, and Ameena would too. I had grown up listening to such opinions about Islam and the West; my father had felt besieged and considered Islam under threat, and Mohammad and I had inherited those views. Ammi felt besieged too, but she did not have the resentment that my father and Mohammad had. She could only relate to specific matters, such as a Palestinian child being shot, when she would curse the Israelis and the Americans for the atrocity, but she would not have abstract or general opinions about the threat to Islam or the duplicity of the West. My father had been different—I suppose you can say that he had transferred his personal resentments to a cultural, even a cosmic, level. Mohammad was like him.

What about me? Strange as it may sound to you, though I had totally believed in what Mohammad and my father said, perhaps there was a bit of my mother in me, too—I had not thought too much in abstract and larger terms. The presence of Ameena in the flat changed that. Ameena brought a bit of her mum to the flat. Like Aunty, Ameena was an intellectual person—a girl who reasoned with concepts, facts, figures, and ideas. For her, a wounded Palestinian boy being carried in the arms of his father was not primarily a human tragedy, an affront to the justice and religion of Allah, which surely Allah would avenge. That, I suppose, was what my Ammi would think, if she thought of it beyond her moment of instinctive sympathy, watching it on TV, and the standard curse that slipped from her mouth, before she returned to her Quran or kitchen. I might give it more thought, but, like Ammi, I would not try to fix it, absolutely, as the conspiracy of a selection of specific villains in the past and the present.

Ameena would. She and Mohammad sat facing the TV for hours, discussing the event, tracing it back to the past, agreeing on everything—how the Russians had invaded Afghanistan and been resisted by the heroic mujahideen, these indomitable Afghan fighters who at the time were supported by the US, which simply wanted more clout in the region, and how these great Afghan heroes had suddenly been branded as the Taliban and as terrorists and were now being bombed by the same US and its allies. They would go on and on, each getting more impassioned with the support of the other. The ghost of hurt that I had detected in Ameena's liquid eyes would change shape and harden into anger or resentment.

That, perhaps, was the difference between her and Mohammad. Mohammad had exactly the same opinions and sometimes even the same words. But the words did not leave him bitter and restless; they left him feeling good and righteous. Again and again, Ameena would conclude by lamenting her ability to do anything to change the world, to protect other Muslims from being attacked by a crass, vulgar West. Mohammad, on the other hand, would end his condemnation of the West and even Muslims—almost all of the other Muslims who did not believe and practise the faith like we did—with a smile of satisfaction, as if this litany of infamy made him feel proud (I might say "smug" today) at being what he was.

Listening to them, and I mostly listened, I felt that they would make a good couple. Yes, the thought crossed my mind. I mentioned it to my mother. She smiled. Did I tease Ameena with the notion? I don't think so; we were very serious girls by then. ("You were born ten years older than anyone else in our class," Ameena used to joke.) We indulged in little frivolous talk, though we still had our girly fits of giggles when the world got too funny. Did the possibility of marrying my brother cross Ameena's mind? I don't know. What I do remember is that she used to be very animated in all her conversations with Mohammad. She evidently took pleasure in his company. But Mohammad never noticed her as a woman. I always know when a man notices a woman; I did even then. It is the kind of instinct some people have more than others. Ameena did not have it, despite all her early escapades, the adult cigarettes and the adult boys she had gone around with. She wanted a man to love her, but she could not tell when a man was interested in her and when he was not. Not then, not later.

***

That summer is the last season I remember as a period of normality. After that, whether it was England or Turkey or Syria, I was swept up in a storm, and it has only started fading away here, in beautiful Bali. Though even now, as we sit here talking, the wind has not died out, the thunder may still crash, and I can cower in the depths of my soul, waiting for lightning to strike and obliterate everything, all those fragments that I daily shore up, as one of Mrs. Chatterji's poets put it, against my ruin. I need to look out on such occasions and focus on the world outside me—small external details help calm the storm, things like that milkwood tree out there, the way sunlight falls on its leaves, the precarious angle at which that small green bird perches on the dry branch there, so that it almost seems to be a leaf.

But that summer all seemed calm to me. I had found a best friend in Ameena; we were inseparable, as I have told you. While I had never missed Abba as much as I had expected to, perhaps because Mohammad so fully stepped into his shoes even before Abba died, the flat had still been full of his memories. There was that armchair he sat in and read the only newspaper—in Urdu—that we subscribed to. There was the Pakistani TV drama that he watched. It had not stopped running. There were his preferred dishes, which my Ammi would still cook out of habit. And there were his opinions, sometimes even his very words, in Mohammad's mouth. There had been moments over the past two years when he seemed to persist, like a ghostly presence, in our small flat. But those moments had grown sparser—the imperceptibly sliding sand—and they finally disappeared altogether for me that summer.

For a time, a sort of balance appeared to be restored to the world, at least in our flat. Ammi pottered around, between her kitchen and her Quran, very rarely visiting a neighbour or receiving a visitor. Mohammad dropped in, sometimes with his cronies—though this was rare, as we had a small flat, and I had to keep purdah from most of Mohammad's mates. So perhaps it was Ameena's presence that ushered in a sense of balance and calm. Despite her hurt and anger at the world, she made the flat fill out. The googling and surfing we did, her discussions with Mohammad—strangely, even my mother took to her, sitting with her, sometimes showing her some lines from the Quran or asking her to interpret them. It was then that I realised that Ammi read the Arabic texts by rote; she did not understand Arabic, which had been taught to me and Mohammad, at all. I should have resented her asking Ameena, whose Arabic was rudimentary; she had never asked me or Mohammad, perhaps because we were her children, and she had never dared ask Abba. But I didn't. Ameena had become like a sister to me.

Do you have such periods too? Periods you feel you could go back to, because you let them pass, you wasted

34

them, not realising how precious they were? Periods you threw away like, how does the line go, like pearls before swine? Periods that, if only you could turn the wheel of time back to them, you would knit and embroider forever into your being, never letting them go?

That summer is the last such period that I remember.

***

It was late September. England was getting back to being drizzly and dreary, but there was still sunshine in our flat. That's how I remember it. Mohammad had just returned from the noon prayers, and he had brought Ali along. Ali was his best friend. They had grown up together. They had gone to the same school. Now Ali drove a cab for the same company as Mohammad. Ali's father was part-owner of the company.

Usually, when Mohammad's cronies came to the flat, I was expected to keep mostly or entirely out of sight. But Ali was different. He had come to the flat from the time he was five or so. We had visited his family and they had visited us for as far back as I recalled. Him I could sit with; he would occasionally eat with us too. That day, he joined us for lunch. Ameena was there too. She was not expected to keep purdah, anyway, and she was still wearing only loose dresses and headscarves—what we called jilbab—even when she went outdoors.

Ali had eaten with us and Ameena in the past, and, as always, the conversation was largely between Ameena, Ali, and Mohammad. I listened. Ammi was mostly in the scullery, attending to the biryani and the firni; we often made some elaborate dish on Fridays.

I think something had happened in Gaza around that time, for the talk was about Israel and Jews. We did not distinguish between Jews and Israelis and Zionists; we had never met any, and for us the terms were interchangeable. So when I say that the talk was about Israelis, about fighting and killing Israelis, I am putting it in a way that would sound less repulsive to you.

Actually, Ameena was the one who spoke of doing something. Ali and Mohammad were content with condemnation. They even, I can say in retrospect, revelled in the resentment and righteousness that the actions of Israel—and there had been some vile action then, let me assure you—enabled them to monopolise. Israel's villainy justified their existence; it explained away not only the failures of the Palestinians but even their own individual failures. It did not cause them—or me in those days—any kind of retrospection or unease. The anger we expressed on such occasions was a very comfortable feeling.

Not for Ameena, I realise now. Even then, she wanted to do something about it. She did not know what. But she was not content with wallowing in righteousness and resentment. While we continued to tuck into Ammi's delicious biryani, Ameena's plate grew cold as she lost herself in the arguments and the discussion.

I recall her saying to the men, with that angry challenge in her eyes: "If A wor a boy, A'd go fight!"

"Fight who?" Ali asked, half-laughingly.

"The Israelis, Assad, Americans, Iranians, whatsamatter with yer? Whoever needs to be smashed," she retorted, shaking a puny fist at him.

"Yup," said Mohammad, "I can see them running scared of

you, Ameena, all four feet, eleven inches of you." We laughed, and soon her scowl changed into a grudging smile as well.

Am I mixing up this occasion with another one? In any case, Ali ate with us and Ameena a number of times, so it might have been the same occasion or a later one. But it was on one of these occasions that Mohammad let drop that he was getting engaged·to Ali's sister. My Ammi had obviously been consulted already, and I know she would have been delighted with the proposal. We had known Ali's family for years; they even came from the same parts as my parents. But neither Ammi nor Mohammad had thought it necessary to discuss the matter with me.

You may not realise the shock of this sudden announcement: see, even though my parents were never very social, and Ammi had become almost a recluse after Abba's death, it was extraordinary for marriages to be fixed without a lot of talk, gossip, discussions. One almost always knew who would be marrying whom at least six months before the betrothal was announced—unless of course it was a runaway romance! The neighbours would know, aunts and cousins would be consulted. And here I, the sister, had no idea: I could imagine that this was one of Mohammad's mosque-inspired ideas, and Ammi had gone along with it. Had she known it for long enough, I would have heard of it. But Mohammad, well, what can I say? My brother always thought he knew best; in some ways he did, in his own eyes. After all, had he not negotiated his two worlds with some success, and often even guided my parents and me? But yes, I was taken aback, though there was no reason they ought to have consulted me. So was Ameena, I could see, even as we hastened to offer our congratulations.

***

Ameena was strangely subdued as we walked to the mosque that afternoon. It was a lecture series by Maulana Abdulaziz—you would have heard of him, the controversial preacher based in Birmingham. He was one of our favourites. I had expected Ameena to be excited—we had never heard Maulana Abdulaziz in person before, though we had watched him on YouTube so often that I can still quote snippets from his speeches: "Have the infidels forgotten the injunction against usury, or do they think that Allah has forgotten them? Not the smallest grain of sand in the depths of the ocean can hide from the sight of the Almighty!" "Some say, 'I will pray only once a day, or I will pray only in my heart, and Allah will forgive me my transgressions.' I say unto them, verily shall you burn in the deepest hell, because you knew and still you disobeyed." "For every inch of your flesh that you show, O unveiled woman who claims she is Muslim, for every inch, O harlot, there are ten devils appointed to lash you in the hereafter." "Would America sit idle if a hundred Jews were killed? Why then do Islamic states sit idle when a thousand Palestinians are slaughtered?"

The mosque was only a short walk from our building. It was on a street forgotten by money, next to a boarded-up pub and a hardware shop that was mostly shuttered. Just before the pub, Ameena stopped suddenly and turned to me. "Jamilla," she asked, "Can A borrow one of yer 'ijabs?"

"Why?" I asked, uncomprehending.

"A can't go to Maulana's do dressed like this," she replied.

We went back. I was at least six inches taller than Ameena, but we were as broad as each other across the hips and shoulders, and I shortened one of my hijabs with pins.

Hijabs and niqabs come in sort of universal sizes anyway. What did you say? One *ummah*? Truly, I would not have smiled in those days; it was deadly serious business for us.

Ameena put on my hijab, and we managed to catch most of Maulana Abdulaziz's lecture at the mosque. After the event, Ameena bought two hijabs for herself: one black and one a dark purple.

***

The next morning, Aunty came to our flat. She was in a dander. I have told you she was a small birdlike woman, usually in a rush, irritated or hassled. At least that is the way I saw her. But I had never seen her angry. She ignored me and asked for my mother. She launched into a tirade even before Ammi had finished, asking her to come in. She spoke about how she had been glad for my friendship with Ameena, as it had removed her from some bad influences and she liked me as a studious, serious girl; she respected other people's faiths and their interpretation of her own faith, but there were limits, and putting a hijab on her daughter had crossed that limit. She would not put up with it.

You have probably formed an idea of my Ammi by now. You can imagine her reaction; she started stuttering and was probably about to apologise on my behalf, without perhaps even fully comprehending what the argument was about, but Mohammad had not left for work yet, and he intervened. Had Mohammad not been there, I suppose Ammi would have mollified Aunty with her submissive acceptance of other people's opinions, her deferential indication that of course she always knew less than anyone else, and Ameena could probably have continued using the hijab outside while making it invisible in Aunty's presence. After all, no one wears a hijab at home! But Mohammad took over, with his male assurance, his obvious air of superiority and correctness in all matters of faith. They argued back and forth for half an hour. Aunty did not have a chance. Looking back, I can see the quandary she was in and sympathise with her: you cannot really discuss a moderate faith with someone who has an immoderate version of it. Any such discussion gets taken over by the person who holds the religious high ground, and you either have to relinquish all claim to faith, which leaves you nowhere in such a debate, or you have to scramble for higher theological grounds, which makes your rational objections disappear or seem unsound. It is a bit like a skirmish between a force in an open valley and fighters occupying the mountainside around it.

Aunty lost the skirmish. I think it made her angrier. She stomped back and had a big argument with Ameena. A reet ding-dong, Ameena called it later. There was shouting and screaming on both sides. The banging of doors, slamming of books. We could hear it. Mohammad smiled grimly at the sounds. My mother shook her head and said, "This place." I felt oddly torn. There was more of it that evening. It continued for a few days. Then an ominous silence descended, and I suspect mother and daughter almost never had a normal conversation after that.

I have said I felt oddly torn—triumphant and guilty at the same time. I did not understand the guilt then, because I was so convinced that Aunty was wrong and Ameena right. There was no doubt in my mind. Why then should I feel guilty? And yet I did; I even resented Mohammad's grim smile. It is only now, in this green Bali with its small Hindu shrines, that I have begun to understand it. Actually, some months ago, when I read Rumi for the first time. Yes, for the first time. Abba or Mohammad had no time for the Sufis. I might have heard of Rumi in school, maybe Mrs. Chatterji could have brought him up some day, but I would not have read him. Abba scoffed even at the Sufi shrines that Ammi sometimes mentioned having visited as a child. So Rumi was a total revelation to me. It was when I was reading this long poem by him that I began to understand why I had felt guilty. See, this is a poem about Prophet Ibrahim—Abraham—encountering an illiterate shepherd who prays to and imagines God—Allah—as if God was a beautiful lamb. Abraham is scandalised. He scolds the shepherd for his mistake, blasphemy and ignorance, and strides away. A bit farther, and the voice of God takes Abraham to task. "What have you done?" the voice of God asks, "A prophet's work is to join hearts to me, not to sunder hearts." Do you understand? That is what I had done: I was no prophet, but I had sundered hearts. Or maybe, if that sounds too melodramatic, I had helped sunder hearts. A mother and her daughter. No wonder I felt a twinge of conscience then. No wonder I cannot go back and face Aunty even today. But I could not have known all that, not in those days. Allah, they seem to be a century ago at times, in another world! I would not even have read such a poem then, and if I had, I would have dismissed Rumi as blasphemous!

Ameena continued to wear the hijabs she had bought; if anything, she started dressing even more conservatively. She bought a couple of niqabs too. It was around that time that the trouble in Syria worsened. I followed it, like all of us did, but for Ameena it was more than just another tragedy in a Muslim country: it was an obsession for her. It distracted her from our final exams, and that might explain why she graduated with much lower grades than me from high school. It might also be that she no longer cared about such matters as grades.

***

Mohammad's wedding had been scheduled for a date after our graduation.

A week before the date, Ameena moved into a flat of her own; a one-bedroom pad just a block away from us. Her father had bought it for her. He came to help her move, though he did not go to Aunty's flat. I had to help Ameena carry her things out. Mohammad had offered to help, but Ameena gave his offer a brusque no. She said other girls would be there to help. In the event, no one turned up and I doubt she had asked anyone in any case: there was just the two of us, and Ameena's father's car, a blue Ford Edge. He waited in the new flat. Ameena drove; I did not have a driving licence. Aunty did not help either. She sat in the kitchen, doing something on her laptop, ignoring us.

It took us two trips; there wasn't that much to move. Back in Ameena's new flat—her father had already bought her a bed and a small sofa set—we reassembled her desk and put her study chair in place. Her father helped us with the unpacking. I wonder now what he thought of his daughter's metamorphosis into an orthodox Muslim, this darkly handsome man with his new cars and stylish suits and an English girlfriend (still "number three," I am sure, from what I glimpsed of her, though Ameena once claimed that he was on "number four" now). He might not have remarked that his daughter, who had once been an avid and quite talented photographer, had left her two cameras behind in Aunty's flat, but surely he must have noticed the rest of it: the tight scarf, the niqab outside, and, as he helped us pack, the books: the books on Palestine and Kashmir, the commentaries on the Quran, the translations of the hadith. These books completely dwarfed Ameena's collection of course texts. I had a Quran and a couple of commentaries, but nothing close to what Ameena had accumulated—and what she had read, from the look of it. Surely he would have noticed them? And the prayer beads, the two prayer rugs, and the lack of all photos and paintings, except a photo of the Holy Kaaba, to hang on the new walls? What is it that made him overlook all these paraphernalia of fundamentalism—as Aunty called it? Was it bitterness and resentment at his ex-wife? Was it a guilty love for the child he had abandoned? Was it selfishness? Was it some hidden kernel of superstition or religiosity in the man, or just the male assumption that his child, being a young woman, would be safer with Islam than with the West? Or was it the hypocritical love of a father who considered the freedoms that he allowed himself, and might have allowed a son, to be unsuitable or dangerous for his daughter?

But I never asked these questions then. I took it for granted that all right-minded people, all right-minded Muslims, in any case, would accept the version of the faith I had grown up practising; the version that Ameena had finally embraced with such fervour and intensity.

***

Mohammad's wedding kept me busy. It was a narrow affair— in keeping with our faith—and shorn of a number of rituals and customs my mother had grown up with. She suggested some of them, of course, most of which were rejected by Mohammad and Ali's parents as perversions of Islam.

"Ours is a simple faith, Ammi; you know it," Mohammad often told her with a forbearing smile. "We just need to believe in God and his last prophet. And just one book, that is it; no useless frills and philosophies."

"But, son," she would half-plead, "This was done in our kasbah. In all Muslim weddings. Even your father had to accept …"

"It was wrong, Ammi. It was not really Islamic. Some illiterate local tradition, that is all. There is no sanction for it in Islam."

She would shake her head with a befuddled smile, accept the superior judgement of her son, as she had accepted the superior judgement of her husband, and retire to her kitchen and Quran. But don't think she was unhappy about the wedding. In her own way, I guess she was—she is—happy. You've said that even if God existed, you could not know the mind of God, for that would be a sacrilege from any religious perspective. Divinity is divinity only to the extent that it exceeds the bounds of human understanding, you said. That was one of the statements that made me think of accosting you here. Well, perhaps, happiness is like that, too: we cannot really understand other people's happiness. Or sorrow.

***

Despite the lack of rituals, and the fact that the wedding was basically performed in the mosque (which was unusual for my Ammi too), there were still things to do. Some rituals were still there, the ones sanctioned by Islam, as we were told, and even some customs—like bridal gifts and the wedding dinner—had to be followed. I had to do most of the shopping. Sometimes, Ammi went along—but often she had to attend to things in the flat (she had started cooking a week in advance), and in any case, she disliked shopping outside the neighbourhood.

I had expected Ameena to help me with the shopping—the gifts for the bride and her family, in particular—but she did not seem to have any time. She had started working in a supermarket, and was also settling down in her flat. There were periods when I could not get her on her mobile at all. It irked me, but then the wedding drew closer and I put it out of my mind.

Ameena came for the nikah ceremony at the mosque. My mother was confused by the notion of anything happening in a mosque, and I discovered that this practice, essential to my lot of dedicated believers, seemed entirely untraditional to her. In our kasbah, weddings took place only in homes, not in mosques, she muttered. We humoured her by talking about the food she had cooked and the clothes we had bought, and ignored her complaint.

The nikah was to be conducted by the legendary Imam Abdul, who was in England that year and had agreed to marry the couple, on a request from Ali's father. Ali's father was—is, probably—highly respected in the community. A cab driver like Abba, he had expanded to start his own service—I have told you that both Mohammad and Ali worked for him—and he was the person who had raised money for our mosque. He was also the chairman of the mosque committee.

He was a successful man, but also someone who had dedicated himself to his faith and community. He was friends with a number of orthodox imams and maulvis, obviously, for he ran the mosque almost single-handedly. And despite what happened to me and Ameena, I still do not consider that a sin. You told me you went to a Roman Catholic school. Would you consider the missionaries who ran the school to be necessarily evil because they believed in their God and religion? I would hope not. I see Ali's father as a person like that; someone driven by his faith to do good, not evil. Unfortunately, though, you are right: not all the maulvis and imams who used his mosque confined themselves to doing good. But, let me be fair to them, they had not set out to do evil.

Imam Abdul was a good example. I had been following his preaching for years now. It had started off with injunctions about faith and doing good, following Islam in order to work for a peaceful and fair world. Inevitably, he had to relate to political and social events. He had gone on to criticise Muslims for their infighting and to berate the West for double standards. Then, slowly, his words had gotten more shrill; his ideas more acrid. By the time he came to perform Mohammad's nikah, he was what you would call a firebrand Islamist.

The nikah is a simple ceremony, as you probably know. Basically, the imam gets the consent of the bridegroom and the bride, and marries them in the presence of witnesses. Afterward, the imam might preach about marriage and the duties of a Muslim. Imam Abdul did. I remember that his sermon slid from the topic of marriage and family life to far more political subjects, causing some of the gathering,

including Ali's father, to mutter that the talk was inappro-
priate for the occasion. Ameena had been there for the talk,
listening with rapt attention. When the talk was finally over
and I mentioned that perhaps, as Ali's father had said, the
revered and learned imam had touched on subjects that were
better broached on some other occasion, Ameena frowned
and replied, "Yes, that is the problem with Muslims." At
first I thought she had agreed to my muffled criticism of the
imam, driven not from any ideological difference but simply
because, like most family members, we wanted to get on
with the wedding ceremonies. But that is not what Ameena
meant. She added, moodily, "We Muslims get more fussed
about what's proper than faith."

Soon afterward, she pleaded a headache—she was prone
to mild bouts of migraine—and excused herself from the
wedding dinner. She had been unpredictable for days now.

AMEENA'S FLAT

Carried away by the idea and the occasion of my brother's wedding, I had not given enough thought to what it would mean. Suddenly, Mohammad's wife—I called her Bhabhi—was in our flat. It was never a big flat. There was a master bedroom, occupied by my parents; my Ammi had stayed there after Abba's death. Then there were two other rooms, smaller ones, which had served as my bedroom and Mohammad's. There was the usual corridor, sitting room, bathroom and kitchen, and a small balcony on one side. That was it.

Ammi vacated the main bedroom for the newlyweds and moved into Mohammad's room. I stayed where I was. But suddenly the flat shrank. In particular, I felt like an intruder in the morning, every time I walked into the bathroom and found my brother and his bride brushing their teeth, and in the evenings, when they would sit together on the sofa to watch a programme. I had started working part-time for a local women's NGO, but that did not give me enough to do, and I often went over to Ameena's flat. She seemed to have more time now; I was almost the only friend she had left. Even many of the faithful girls, the ones we knew from our mosque meetings, did not drop in too often. Around that time, Ameena and I dismissed them as giddy-headed types, but looking back I realise that Ameena's bitter diatribes against the apathy of Muslims and the villainy of the West had probably become too much for them.

One evening, we sat in Ameena's flat watching news on the TV that Aunty, in one of her irregular bids to build bridges, had gifted us some days ago. We had a bowl of chips and some Coke in front of us. The news was not too bad that evening. No Muslim was being blamed for a terror strike, and no Palestinian boy or Afghan girl had been killed on purpose or by mistake. Ameena must have been in a good mood.

"Why don't yer move in with me, Jamilla?" she asked all of a sudden.

I laughed, helping myself to more chips.

"No, seriously," she said, "A mean it. Don't yer get wearied stiff of the company of that sweet lil sis-in-law of yours? Move in tomorrer."

"I don't get to see her that often, Ameena," I replied, "I spend more time with you."

"A don't know what A'd do if A'd to share a pad with a gal who can't go out because 'er nail-polish clashes with t'colour of 'er 'ijab!"

I smiled. Bhabhi had some curious habits; she had grown up with more affluence. What surprised me was that Mohammad put up unconditionally with her mix of fashion with faith. He even took fond pride in it.

***

A few days must have passed since this conversation when I mentioned Ameena's offer to my family. I did so at a meal, probably as part of some light conversation, unthinkingly. I was surprised to see that both Mohammad and Bhabhi took the offer seriously. I hadn't, until that moment.

Bhabhi and Mohammad started discussing its advantages. "She'd be near us and with her best friend," said Bhabhi. "I can give you a monthly allowance," added Mohammad. He mentioned a sum that was exactly half of what my mother contributed to the household from the insurance payments she received. Before my bemused eyes, it was all settled. You might laugh now, but once it was settled, I found it the most natural option of all. I did not think, then, that it offered some obvious advantages to my brother and sister-in-law. That realisation came much later. They might not have been aware of it either. And in my case, I suspect, I was so used to accepting all the decisions of my father and then my older brother as inevitable, that once this decision had been taken, it too appeared to be the most normal, the most natural of all options to me.

I remember ringing Ameena right there, from the table, and asking her if she really wanted me to move in with her. She was overjoyed. After many years, I heard her shriek with joy like she used to when we had first met. A girly shriek, the sort that they do in stupid teenage TV serials, when they hold hands and hop around, shrieking. I never did that, of course. Ameena had stopped years ago. But I heard that shriek over the mobile then. It was the last time I heard it from Ameena.

***

Living with Ameena was not too different from living at home, except that we had more time and freedom. We bought another bed, and put it against the opposite wall in her room. This left us with just a narrow passage in between the beds, but we had our spacious sitting room, and I no longer felt like an intruder going to the bathroom to brush my teeth in the mornings.

The only conflict, a minor one, I had with Ameena was when I started to put up my only poster in our shared bedroom. I had grown up with it: three kittens playing with a ball of wool. Ameena objected to it. She did not have any picture of an animal or a human—or an idol, obviously—on her walls. But this childhood poster of three cuddly kitlins? What harm could it do? It was not as if we would confuse the kittens with a deity or a prophet and start worshipping them. Even my father had never objected to the poster. But Ameena was adamant. "This is how it starts," she argued, "This is the thin edge o' idolatry: from fetish to idol to false gods." I could not really argue against her, though I felt, even then, that it was unnecessary. I also realised that Ameena had gone further than me. I was slightly irked and hugely impressed. The poster stayed in my bag.

Our routine did not change much. We had our work during the daytime. Ameena worked longer hours than I did. I would spend my hours alone in the flat preparing for or planning a college career. Ameena, whose parents expected her to go to university, had no plans to study further, but I, whose mother was dead against any further education and had already mentioned marriage, did plan to study. I just did not know what to study and how to go about it. I also did not know how to face my Ammi and brother with the news that for now I wanted to study, not get married.

When Ameena returned, we usually spent time cooking, watching TV, or, increasingly, chatting with our friends on the Internet. As our friends in real life had diminished after school, our friends on the Internet had grown in number. There was little we shared with our ex-school friends any more. They were obsessed with fashions and boys and films;

Ameena and I were more interested in matters of faith and life, as we saw it. They dressed in ways that embarrassed us, except for a couple of the Muslim girls; and we obviously dressed in a manner that made many of them feel uncomfortable. I had not noticed it as much before Ameena started putting on the niqab. Of course, there had been the occasional comment or rude remark—less often by a schoolmate than by some total stranger in the supermarket. But I had been wearing the hijab from the time I turned thirteen (and the niqab only a few years later)—not that we had cut a cake to mark it, as my father considered birthday celebrations a Western custom—and perhaps I had not noticed the difference in the way some people looked at me after I started veiling myself. In any case, I noticed it only after Ameena put on the niqab and brought such occasions, some real, some assumed, to my attention.

Perhaps the year after you finish high school is a lonely one for all students; suddenly you have been forced out of the cocoon of school life and your wings are still too weak to enable you to fly anywhere. In our case it could have been worse. The few mosque friends we had would not have sufficed. Luckily, there was the Internet—and an entire world out there in which we were the norm, not the exception.

Did I say out there? No, some of them were in England, even in our city. We met and became friends with two or three women through such Internet chats. But it is true: most of them seemed to be elsewhere. And most of them seemed to be doing something about the issues that exercised us. Ameena and I identified with all of them, erasing the differences that existed with the brush of a hypothetical Islam, an imagined community. I am sure most of them did the same. But what, I wonder now, did we really have in common with the Somalian girl who refused to read anything but the Quran, the Algerian girl whose Islamism was driven by colonial memories of French atrocities instead of any firm religious belief, the Palestinian woman who had given up on moderate politics because she was convinced that Israeli and American politicians were lying about the two-state solution, or, for that matter, green-eyed Michelle, a stunning nineteen-year-old brunette from a Parisian suburb, a self-confessed "film buff" who had converted to Islam after an online romance with a jihadi she had not even met, and who was daydreaming of a future fighting by his side: she saw him as a modern-day Robin Hood and once told us that her favourite "Hollywood oldie" was *Bonnie and Clyde*. "Film barmpot," Ameena had quipped, and we had laughed ourselves silly, while at the same time loving this naïve Parisian with sculpted eyebrows and full lips for joining our fight. What fight? Whose fight? We never really asked such questions.

Of these fellow "fighters," the woman Ameena took to most of all was at least a decade older than us, but had grown up in Wales as a child. Then her parents—Kuwaitis—had moved back to Kuwait, and from there to Saudi Arabia. She had married an Arab computer programmer who had quit his job, first to join some Arab political uprising with vaguely democratic aspirations, and then to gradually move toward jihadist groups. Now, she claimed, he was fighting for the "faith" in Syria, and she was there to support him, which was the job of all women—to help their men fight for the faith.

She used to go by the Twitter name of Hejjiye, a word that means "pilgrim" and is usually employed to refer to old women in parts of Arabia. For all I know, she might still be around on Facebook and Twitter. I would not care to find out now.

***

Hejjiye was completely involved in the insurrection in Syria. She posted accounts of the bravery of jihadists and the knavery of the regime forces and the so-called secular opposition. Sometimes the information she—and others like her—posted was at variance with what the Western media reported. You would imagine that such discrepancies would have discredited her in our eyes. By no means! Ameena and I had no trust in the Western media: we saw them, and even today I feel that there was an element of truth in our perception, as "embedded" reporters, catering to their governments' requirements in most cases and blinded by their own cultural assumptions in almost everything. Perhaps, on our own, Ameena or I would have thought about it, and divided up the falsehoods and truth equally between the two sides. But we were not on our own. We sustained each other's assumptions; we fed them. The discrepancies and contradictions in the accounts of people like Hejjiye seemed to be proof of their veracity in our eyes. We were fascinated by such women—and men, for we occasionally corresponded with male Islamists, too, and followed the postings of at least a couple of male jihadists. It was much easier in those days; ISIS or *ad-Dawlah al-Islamiyah fi 'l-'Iraq wa-sh-Sham*—I prefer the term Daesh now (how Hejjiye would hate it!)—was barely a rumour, and the rumour had not carried to the Western media yet.

Once or twice, I attempted to get my brother and his wife interested in following some of these people, and in particular Hejjiye. Hejjiye wrote good English; she was a strikingly beautiful woman. I thought my brother would appreciate her views, which tallied with his: Muslims under attack, the duplicity of the West, the lack of faith of Muslims, the role of a wife, the decency expected from women, etc. And Bhabhi would surely ooh and aah over the photos with her dusky Chartreux cat, Batala ("heroine" in Arabic), or her collection of Gucci handbags that Hejjiye sometimes posted. But Mohammad and Bhabhi did not seem to have time for all this.

Mohammad, I knew, was like my father. They did not take to pets, and the only time when, as a girl of eleven or twelve, I had obtained a mewling spotted kitten from a school friend, I had been asked to return it—as "there was no space in the flat." That might have been the last time I had thrown a tantrum, running away into my room, slamming the door, and crying into a pillow, until Ammi had managed to distract me with freshly fried savouries and the promise to get a cat once we moved to a bigger place. We were always moving to a bigger place in those days. Bhabhi, however, used to have a cat—I recalled how much I envied her every time we visited Ali's family. I thought she would notice Hejjiye's cat, a beautiful breed, a species that was native to Syria—see, I had spent years reading up on the cats I could not keep! Did you know that Syria is the place where cats were domesticated for the first time? It is the land of cats! I knew all this even when I was twelve. The few photos that Hejjiye had posted of her dusky "heroine," Batala, endeared her to me. I will concede that. How can you not love a cat-lover? Just as Bhabhi's disinterest in Hejjiye's cat photos made me feel that I had less to say to the women in my own family than perhaps I would to someone like Hejjiye.

***

Now that I had moved out of the flat, Bhabhi had estab-
lished a kind of tradition of inviting me over to have lunch
or dinner every Friday. She would also invite Ameena, but
Ameena mostly found reasons not to join me. On the few
occasions that she came along, she did so only because I
insisted, as it was a festival or we had something to celebrate.
The last time was toward the end of Ramazan: the month-
long fasting had left us tired, and we were expecting to
have news of the new moon that evening or the next. I had
insisted she joined us for the iftar.

You would know that there are various ways in which
Muslims break the fast. Most orthodox Muslims do so by
drinking a glass of water and eating a date or two, after which
they say the prayer, and then they return to eat a full meal.
We had grown up believing that this was the right method:
you break the fast with a date or two, say the prayer, and
then return to eat properly. But at least in this matter, we
did not follow the orthodox way. Ever since I could recall,
we would have a small dish, a kind of starter—usually a
samosa or something like that, along with the dates and the
refreshing drink. Then, thirst and hunger partly assuaged,
we would say the *namaz* and return for a full meal.

Ameena objected to this. She had by then, even to me,
started resembling Aunty. Some of it had to do with her
losing weight. But most of it was due to her habit of pointing out flaws and ticking people off. This was particularly
pronounced in matters of religion. Ameena knew very little
Arabic—she was working on it. Mohammad and I had been
taught Arabic, and we read it and even spoke it with some
fluency. But Ameena, like most Muslim children, had only

been taught to read the Quran, more or less by rote. In order to understand it, she had to take recourse to translations in Urdu or English. And perhaps because of this, she was a stickler for very narrow interpretations of the text; she did not allow much space for dissension.

Not that we disagreed. But even I found it a bit irritating when she refused to take a morsel other than a date—"Surely, 'tis wrong t' keep Allah waiting just 'cause you're a mite hungry," she said—even as Bhabhi bit into her first samosa, having polished off a few dates. Then Ameena picked up a prayer mat and went to a clean space to say her namaz. Bhabhi frowned and put down her samosa. There was nothing we could do. We felt wrong-footed in our own faith; we felt inordinately greedy. We had to follow Ameena's example and say our prayers first, with just a date and a slurp of water in us.

Half an hour later, when we were all finally at the table, eating, I could see from the colour on Bhabhi's face that she was irritated at Ameena. There had been little love lost between the two. But despite Ameena's often acrid comments, Bhabhi continued to be polite. She was not a woman who took offence very readily. But this evening, Ameena had gone too far with her.

Did your parents—I can safely assume *you* don't fast—have a set menu for the iftar? They did, didn't they? We had a set menu too. And we always ended with some kind of lemonade and a mix of sliced and cubed fruit, lightly sugared and spiced. We usually took our bowls of fruit and glasses of lemonade to the sofa and watched the news, even though my Ammi would leave us then to start reading her Quran. We did so that evening too.

The news was switched on. It was Syria or Iraq. Or maybe it was Palestine, some outbreak in Gaza. Or perhaps even Afghanistan. Strange, isn't it, I do not recall clearly any longer. But you can imagine what it must have been. And because it was one of those topics on which she often posted, I asked Bhabhi and Mohammad if they had checked out our Internet friend and guide Hejjiye lately.

"Ameena's become such good friends with Hejjiye that sometimes I feel jealous," I joked.

Bhabhi frowned and said, addressing her husband, "I did check her once. She seems to be quite a martyr, doesn't she? Very smug, with a polished gun in one arm and a stray cat in the other!"

Mohammad muttered, noncommittal. I wanted to defend Hejjiye's cat—it is a Chartreux, I felt like saying, and in any case, what if it is a stray?—but Ameena took offence faster than me.

"What do yer mean?" she asked, "Hejjiye's out there, fighting for all of us with her 'usband."

"Oh yes," replied Bhabhi, looking her in the eye, "That is what she says."

"An' what do yer think?"

"I think you should only believe what you see with your own eyes."

"So, go there!" challenged Ameena.

"Go where?"

"Go t'Syria, t'Iraq, t'Afghanistan. Go and see with yer own eyes, instead of just believing what the Western media tells yer, like, like all the old farts around us!"

"I do not believe all that the British media tells me," Bhabhi protested.

"What do yer believe then?" Ameena continued. Then she turned to my brother, "An' yer? What do yer believe?"

"I believe what you believe, Ameena," Mohammad had replied, not really getting Ameena's point.

"Why don't yer go and fight then?" asked Ameena, "You know t' 'oly Quran as well as A do. Yer know it says: Allah shall grant to t'jihadis above t'holders back a mighty reward."

"The 'strivers,' it says in the holy book, Ameena, not jihadis, as you put it," Muhammad corrected her.

"Yer know it means t'same thing," Ameena shot back.

"Maybe. I strive in my own way."

"How?" Ameena scoffed, "Mohammad Bhai strives by preaching to t'drunks he drives around ev'ry weekend!"

Mohammad laughed, shamefacedly.

But Bhabhi shot back: "And what do you do?" she asked, "What do you do, Ameena, in a flat bought for you by your father, who doesn't even live like a good Muslim?"

There was a moment of silence. We felt—and I am sure Bhabhi felt so, too, judging from the expression on her face—that the argument had gone too far. The conversation then drifted, as it does on such occasions, into neutral areas, as if no breach had occurred.

But I heard Ameena say in a small, tight voice, "You're raight."

***

That might have been when the germ of the idea set in Ameena's mind. I did not discover it until later. Not that Ameena hid anything from me; she shared her Internet correspondence with me and often spoke of the issues that they raised. When a man who claimed to be a jihadi offered to marry her, she showed me the offer with a laugh, too. So perhaps it wasn't Ameena. Perhaps it was me. Around that time I was busy exploring options for higher education.

I had been a good student, though not an excellent one. All through school I had been good at subjects that needed memorisation, like biology and history. But I was never one of the best students. This did not matter in the case of students like Alex, who obviously had parents who could pay and advise. I did not. I could have asked Aunty, but it never crossed my mind. Ameena used to avoid her mum—their last spat had been over Ameena's refusal to consider college—and so did I, unthinkingly. My Ammi, not having completed school, was no help. Mohammad had stopped after high school and considered higher education a waste. Bhabhi stayed noncommittal on the matter, perhaps fearing that it would impose an extra expenditure on them.

My only options were my ex-school friends. Unlike Ameena, I had stayed in touch with some, especially James and the Muslim girls. James was already studying literature. I consulted them. I went out to a few places with them to check out options. Ameena refused to come along. One day when James insisted on visiting us in the flat with his Caribbean girlfriend, Ameena hardly sat with them, claiming a migraine. Later, she berated me for letting "someone as dirty as James" come into a room where we pray. I protested that James was a bit unkempt, true, but by no means dirty. She shut me up with two rapid questions: "Yer think they don't drink or eat pork? Yer think he washes after peeing?" she asked, sounding exactly like her mum when Aunty got upset. Then she had both of us change all the sheets that could be changed and wipe the table.

So perhaps it was me. I was busy trying to work out
my life. And it was difficult. My mother and Mohammad
were not hostile to the idea of higher education for me; they
were simply indifferent. I might as well have been building a
model plane. It was obvious to me that I could start studying
only if I got some kind of scholarship. I could not possibly
ask them to support me; I was not even sure they could have
afforded it. A study loan could not be considered: I am sure
Mohammad would have objected to it on grounds of interest. I found the idea of interest alien and un-Islamic too. The
other option would be to keep working for years and save up
or study on the side. But that sounded difficult and uncertain. So, with the help of my few friends, I tried to narrow
down my applications to a couple of places, all within commuting distance, where I hoped I would be offered some
sort of scholarship, perhaps not enough to cover everything
but enough to afford me the strength that I needed to strike
out on my own. You see, there was very little choice for me.
Not just in terms of where I could study, but also what.
Only subjects such as pharmacy and computer science,
it seemed, would allow me reasonable financial prospects
without interfering with my religious practices, or would
enable me to work in a relatively secluded setting without
exposing myself to strangers or spending time alone with
men I did not know. There weren't that many options.

***

I had just posted my applications when my Ammi dropped
her bomb. She had called and asked me to stop by. By then,
I was working almost full-time as a clerk in a corner shop. I
dropped in after finishing work.

Ammi bustled about brewing tea, even though I told her I would make it. "Not today," she replied.

We sat on the sofa and sipped the tea. As always, Ammi had put too much sugar in it. I did not say anything. Ammi leaned over and tilted my face a bit, holding me by the chin, as you would a child.

"I had never noticed it, but my baby has grown into a beautiful woman," she said. She got up and fetched an envelope. She shook out its contents onto the sofa between us. Three photos and a letter, in Urdu, fell out. She took up the biggest photo: it featured a family, the parents sitting stiffly on chairs, and two sons and two daughters standing behind them. It had been taken in a garden with the back of a house showing behind them. "That's their house in Birmingham," said my Ammi. Then she took up the other two photos. Both of them featured a sallow-looking, pudgy young man wearing expensive glasses and dressed in an embroidered kurta in one photo and in a suit and tie in the other. "That is their youngest son, Iskandar. He is CA."

I am not sure Ammi knew what CA was. She looked expectantly at me. I still did not understand her.

She went away again. I noticed how thin and old she had grown, how she had started to hunch a bit, and her feet dragged when she walked, the rubber slippers making a rustling-slapping sound. She came back with a blue velvet-covered box about the size of an iPad but thicker. She put it on my lap and opened it. It contained her jewellry, mostly gold and silver necklaces and earrings. "This one," she said, picking out the heaviest necklace, "I got for my wedding." She held it for a second, rapt. Then she said a few things about some of the other pieces, finally dismissing the smaller ones with the remark that those were what she had bought whenever she could save a bit of money, because gold and silver are good to invest in. "Though I guess these are not worth much," she added.

All of what she had shown me was not worth much either, though I guess it did have a combined value of maybe four thousand pounds.

"I have kept all these for your wedding," she said.

It was then that I understood. But I pretended not to understand. One part of me must have been hoping that the notion would go away, as so many suggestions do, if one simply ignored it.

But Ammi went on: "They were there, don't you remember, at Mohammad's wedding. The father is a cousin of Ali's mother. They saw and liked you there at the wedding. They sent this proposal last week through Ali's mother."

Before I could say anything, Ammi added, "It is such a good match. They are religious people, good people; they even have two cars. And, once you are married, I can die in peace."

"Surely, Ammi, you have no plan of dying!" I joked, hugging her.

She disentangled herself and held me affectionately. Her eyes were brimming with tears. "Your father, Allah bless him, always wanted to leave behind more for you than we could. But this boy and his family, I am sure they will give you all the comforts we could not provide you with. You know, it is unusual for a boy's people to approach the girl's family. It would never be done in my kasbah when I was a girl. Just shows how much they like you. They are good, modern people; religious too."

"But, Ammi," I pouted, "I have always had everything I wanted."

She patted my head, sadly.

***

I went back to Ameena's flat in a thoughtful mood. Ammi had given me to understand that there was no hurry; the boy's people were willing to wait two or three months for our reply.

Three months seemed like a big rush to me! I had not thought of marriage. Not one of the girls from my class had married yet. Some of them were living with partners, but these were not Muslim girls. Marriage had been something like the rumour of a distant war; now, suddenly, the cannons were at my doorstep. I did not know what to do, and simply hoped that one of my applications would get me a scholarship. I knew that Ammi might not like it, but she would not object to my decision to study further—if there was a scholarship attached to it. Neither would Mohammad. His wife did have a college degree. And if Ammi did mind, I was sure I could talk her around it; I could postpone the marriage by two or three years, until I got my degree, and if the boy's people liked me so much, surely they would accept it. You see, I had nothing against getting married to the boy. All my life I had been groomed to marry a man like him. It is just that the idea of getting married right now sent me into a kind of panic.

Oh, how I prayed for one of my applications to be successful!

***

The next evening, as we peeled potatoes for dinner, I showed the photo of my prospective bridegroom to Ameena. She found it funny, and warned me: "A've seen this sort of thing at me aunt's in Chicago. The next time your mum will want yer t'dress properly." Then we looked at each other and the same thought struck us—I had dressed properly for years and now even Ameena always did. Choking on her words, Ameena dropped the peeler into the sink. We burst out laughing. Then, wiping tears of laughter from her eyes, Ameena suddenly asked, "You want t'meet me groom?"

I was taken aback. "I didn't know Aunty's been talking to you about getting married!" I exclaimed.

"She isn't," Ameena laughed, "It'd give me mam a 'eart attack if A talked about getting married off now. She wants me to get a university degree. Me Abba too. Says he'll pay for it. Set 'im back a suit or two, A dare say!"

I resumed peeling a potato and looked at her.

She winked, mischievously.

"Don't tell me you're dating someone, Ameena!" I said, horrified.

She looked miffed. "Do yer think A'm so … so dumb, Jamilla? You'll start dating sooner'n me! Yer love it when boys look at yer!" she barked.

I denied it.

"They do look at yer, yer know," she insisted.

I knew they did, but I argued that they did not: how could they when I was always veiled in public?

"They notice yer, veil or not veiled," she noted. Then she relented, adding, "No, A am not dating; A never will. Yer know A'd never cut corners on me faith."

"But …" I murmured. I was confused.

"A might tell yer more someday," she said, mysteriously.

***

One by one the results of my applications came in. I was given admission in one place, but there was no scholarship, no funding of any sort. Ammi was pressing me for an answer to the proposal. I had to take up the matter with her and my brother. I arranged to talk to them after dinner one evening.

I explained to them that I did want to get married and would be happy to marry the boy from Birmingham, of course, but I wished to study a bit more too. They were not against my ambitions, but they did not know how I could continue my education. Where was the money? Would a good boy wait that long? I felt these were reasonable objections.

Bhabhi was there too, but she did not say much. Toward the end, she suggested that perhaps I could meet the boy and his people and discuss it with them. "It is common for girls to study after getting married now," she noted.

My mother was displeased with the idea of a meeting. It had never been done in her kasbah. But Mohammad assured her that, as long as the requirements of purdah were maintained, it was not against the faith. Bhabhi promised to talk to her parents about it.

I walked back to Ameena's flat in a depressed mood. There did not seem to be any option; this way or that it appeared that I had to marry soon; this boy or that, it hardly mattered. The streets seemed filled with tawdriness and noise. I turned down an alley. A group of smartly dressed young people—a flurry of high-waisted denim shorts and flowing white tops, of pumped-up kicks and boots, of Fred

Perry polo shirts and blazers from Gap—passed by on their way to a pub or a party. At least a couple of them were Indian or Pakistani. One of them glanced at me and then looked away, pointedly. I felt out of place there. I had grown up in this neighbourhood, but it was not home. I did not belong here, I felt; I never would. The idea of continuing to live a version of this life in Birmingham did not appeal to me. The idea of living it with that vapid, satisfied-looking man in the photo frightened me. I stepped over the garbage, walking faster, my shadow being split into many shadows by the lights on the streets and from the shuttered shop-fronts.

I think that was the moment when I first felt the burn of resentment at Mohammad and Bhabhi—and in the beginning even at poor Ammi. How easily all of them had disinherited me! They had not done it consciously, surely, but then neither had this city. Did it matter? After all, I was just as homeless in my father's flat that, by rights, belonged to me too, as I was in this city. Of course, I had legal claims on both the flat and the city, but legal claims were not enough for me. I throttled the thought; the burn persisted. You might think I am a hard-hearted girl, but it would have been different if legal claims had sufficed for me—a third share of the flat according to Islam, or full voting rights in the city according to my passport. Oh, it would all have been different. But to live only by dry legal claims? What kind of an impoverished life would that be? Perhaps it is those who are most vulnerable in their hearts who learn to grow the toughest skin.

***

Ameena was surfing when I got in. She was chatting with Hejjiye, who had been posting mysteriously about a great victory for Islam. Her husband had been made a commander, and one of her three co-wives had just given birth. But she was mostly excited about recent Daesh victories. "We are cutting through the infidels and the traitors like a hot knife through butter," she wrote. Her English was colloquial.

See, Jamilla, see, what a cute little baby, Ameena said, and in passing I caught a wrinkled pink thing wrapped in green cloth on her screen. But I had a headache building up. I went to my bed and lay there.

Ameena kept shouting out the news to me, mixing up Daesh victories with Hejjiye's domestic matters. It was only after some time that Ameena noticed I was not responding to her enthusiasm. Usually, I would. She shut down her laptop and came over to me.

"Something wrong, Jamilla?" she asked, sitting on the edge of my bed. I told her. She listened, without interrupting, which was unusual for her. Then she got up suddenly and came back with her laptop. Oh no, I thought, she was not even listening; now, she is going to share some news or opinion with me!

But that is not what she had in mind. She opened her Facebook page and clicked onto one of her Facebook friends. The photo was that of a man, probably in his late thirties, with a checkered scarf hiding one side of his face, shading his eyes. He had a long face, not unhandsome, with strong cheekbones and a curly beard. Behind him there seemed to be a ruin.

"This is Hassan," said Ameena, "He is me bridegroom."

I sat up. His beard was speckled with grey. He wore a magazine carrier with pockets for grenades, and a gun—"a scoped M4 rifle," Ameena informed me, "his favourite weapon"—was slung at his side. Black patches with white Arabic writing adorned the sleeves of his uniform. In his hand, he held a large dagger with a dark blade.

He was not smiling. Hassan seldom smiled.

***

Looking back, it all seems so obvious. Hejjiye had been urging women to join the faithful as wives in the holy fight. Women have a role to play in the jihad too, she would tweet or post. The role was that of wife or mother, but it was the role allotted by Allah, and surely what work could match work given to you by Almighty God! Then, if you were the wife of a martyr, you would be taken care of all your life. To be fair, there were always these men—claiming to be jihadis (who knows what they really were?)—who would approach me on Facebook or on one of the chat pages, urging me to marry them and help usher in the kingdom of God on earth—even if, according to one of them, it would last for just seven years. I would ignore them. I had unfriended one or two, when they got too importunate. They did not seem to me to be very different from the men who would accost me in school and outside it, convinced that if only I went to bed with them, I would discard my dark veil and come to see the light of civilisation. I was slightly scandalised. "But Ameena," I blurted out, "You cannot trust one of these guys."

"What do yer mean?" she demanded.

"How do you know that he is what he claims to be?"

She laughed. "He is not just anyone. He was introduced to me by Hejjiye."

That silenced me; I trusted Hejjiye too. Over the months, she had become like a family member, mixing her political and religious commentaries with news about the illness of the children in her family, or some dish she was going to cook, or worries about her husband who was out on a sortie. At times, she made me wish I had a mother—or an older sister—like her.

Ameena shut her laptop. She said to me, "Ask Hejjiye. She will find yer a good groom too. Not one of these flabby types who talk religion and do nowt; someone who's willing to live t'right way and to fight for t'right cause. Yer know, Hassan wor with *Jabhat an-Nusrah li-Ahli ash-Shām*; but now he's with *them*."

"But you can never marry Hassan, Ameena," I pointed out. "He does not live here."

"There are ways; A've looked," she replied mysteriously. It was obvious to me that Ameena was not telling me everything. It would have worried me, and it was not as if I did not have enough worries of my own.

***

I had hoped the meeting brokered by Bhabhi would take a month or two to arrange, giving me time to work out some strategy or for Allah to intervene in all his mercy. After all, the boy and his family lived in Birmingham. They were busy people. Surely, it would take them a few weeks, maybe a few months, to organise a trip to our town?

I was mistaken. The dinner was organised at Bhabhi's parents' place the very next weekend.

Ammi insisted that I dress up for the occasion, though I would be in purdah with all the men. Ameena wanted to come, but both Bhabhi and Ammi insisted that this would be impossible. Instead, I was encouraged to take the day off and spend it at Ali's and Bhabhi's parents' house, helping out with the cooking. I knew that the best dishes I had helped prepare would be passed off as solely my creation. I went along with all of it. I was the kind of woman who went along in such matters. I had gone along all my life!

The men ate first. We could overhear them talk. The boy had a loud voice. He had strong opinions. He reminded me a lot of Mohammad, my brother, but without that hidden streak of consideration, perhaps visible only to a sister, that redeemed Mohammad and made him likeable. Obviously, better education, more privileges, and a better job had given the boy more confidence. I did not like the sound of his voice.

One of his sisters, a few years older than me, had brought along her children. There were three. A boy of seven or eight and a girl about a year younger, who bickered and bothered their mother until she talked them into crossing over to the men's side; in ten minutes or so, they would be returned to us, no doubt similarly encouraged. The process fascinated me, so automatic it was on the part of the mother. But what frightened me most was her third child: a baby at the suckling stage, alternately mewling or somnambulant throughout the evening. I could not imagine myself with one such, no, not so soon.

The women ate next. I was seated opposite my prospective mother-in-law. She was a large, heavy-set woman—two of my mother could have fitted into her, and there would have been some space left over. She kept praising my looks but did not compliment me on my cooking, half-fictitious though it was. I did not know what to say to her. I spoke very little. I don't think she wanted me to speak. When Bhabhi brought up my desire to study further, my prospective mother-in-law was very understanding and effusive.

"Of course," she said, "Girls want to study these days."

Then she added, "Though a year into your marriage all that nonsense gets forgotten. I know what I am talking of. I had a BA degree when I got married, and now I do not even know where I put my certificates." She laughed loudly. Everyone laughed.

A kitlin scraped its claws on the glass door leading out to the landing. Bhabhi's cat had left descendants. Her parents looked after two or three now. I got up to let in the cat. It was bluish grey with copper eyes, a common British domestic cat, probably a mixed breed, but with the pedigreed Shorthair genes embedded somewhere in its recent heritage. It reminded me of Hejjiye's Batala. Not surprising that it did, of course: I knew that British domestic cats are descended from Syrian and Egyptian ones. I picked it up and cuddled it.

The kitlin gave me a moment to think on my own. Was this how I was going to end: another version of my Ammi? Was that all I could do with my life in this world where there was so much that called out to be done? Was all my reading and piety to end in a kitchen, denying the role that a woman of true faith had to play in this life for which all of us, men in their ways, women in theirs, would have to submit a full account to Allah? Why was it that even such a simple act (holding a cat and feeling it curl into me and purr) left me with a greater feeling of fulfilment than this entire party, than all those family dinners at my brother's flat?

I went back to Ameena's pad with a splitting headache.

***

It is not that people had not objected to my garb before, but the very next morning, as I went to my part-time job, an old woman berated me for being dressed the way I was. She was wearing an antique gown of some sort and was holding an unbelievingly large and flowery bonnet. She might well have been half-crazy. She did not sound like she was from the region. But she stood next to me in the bus and berated me for letting down my gender and not fitting into the culture. People looked uncomfortable and moved away, but no one said anything to stop her. Neither could I.

When I finally got off—a stop early—she shouted after me: "Yew are le'in' down all women, yew idiot."

It helped me make up my mind.

THE FLIGHT

Despite our nervousness, Istanbul's Ataturk Airport was not a problem. We tried not to look chuffed at the success of our plan. We walked leisurely through the steely white interior of the airport, and to the "Visa" sign, white on blue, where we were momentarily stuck behind a gaggle of Chinese or Japanese tourists, one of whom had a slight problem with his papers and had to be talked through by their tour guide. When it was our turn, no one looked at our British passports even twice. "First time here?" the woman at the counter asked me. Then she added, "Sultanahmet, that is the first place to go," almost as if she was quoting from a tourist guidebook. I felt strangely at home as we stepped out of the airport; the Turkish women around us were dressed in ways that ranged from Saudi-orthodox to a fairly good imitation of Alex's cool girlfriends, which (I must shamefacedly confess) drew our hissed and murmured scorn.

We had some time to kill, and I suggested going to the Blue Mosque, but Ameena no longer had time for such frivolous activities as sightseeing—she was entirely focused on what we then considered the "soul" of Islam, to the gross neglect of its body. Or maybe she was more nervous than me; you see, I had the clearer conscience. Ameena, on the other hand, was smuggling in a small packet, marked in Chinese, made in China, which she had guiltily tried out some weeks ago in our now abandoned flat: it was a packet containing artificial hymens. There was no way she could take the risk of her jihadi bridegroom discovering that she was not a virgin. Ameena was tortured by the duplicity: she saw it as a kind of eternal punishment for her un-Islamic ways in the past, this inevitable deception on which she had to build a life of purity and submission, a new life as a good and devout Muslim wife. She marched us to our rendezvous, unwilling to deviate an inch from the plan. She was anxious to leave her past behind. Ameena had taken the precaution of getting one of her cameras from her mum's flat. She slung it prominently around her neck—"Hejjiye said we need to look like tourists," she told me, even buying a tourist guide book for the entire region, which she had tucked, half-visible, into a pocket of her handbag. We had waxed, hooded jackets with contrasting toggles (pale blue for me; light green for Ameena), bought in London, over our hijabs. But she need not have bothered: we were invisible in that mixed crowd, with women in niqabs, in scarves, and in various other dresses, almost everything worn around the Mediterranean, down to short skirts and pantyhose.

Yes, it was August by the time we finally left England. After that betrothal dinner, whose account I had given to Ameena as soon as I returned to her flat (despite my headache), Ameena became more forthright. She told me that she was organising with Hejjiye and some others to join Hassan in Syria. Why don't I go with her?

I hesitated, tempted by the promises, the vision of joining a righteous fight, of doing my duty as a Muslim, of having a purpose in my life; I hesitated, tempted but unsure. You might wonder how I could be tempted. Sometimes I wonder too, today. But the idea had its attractions to a woman like me. I had grown up in a family where the men complained relentlessly about the compromises to their faith that living in England entailed. Daesh had already swept through much of Iraq and was beginning to get bad publicity in the West, but that is what I considered it: bad publicity. Ameena and I, we discussed it for hours. We had Internet friends who agreed with us. Hejjiye was by no means the only person from "over there" who sent us news that contradicted some of what we read or heard in England. We were far from convinced, then, that the Western media was being objective or factual. We were not unusual in this. Most of the Muslims I knew had such doubts, then, even the ones who did not support the declaration of a caliphate by Daesh. Honestly, even people like James had such doubts.

You smile. But you are a man; I don't know if you believe in Allah or you don't, let alone the extent of your faith, but trust me, no man, no Muslim man, no matter how believing, how faithful, how orthodox, has to face a third of the difficulties that orthodox Muslim women encounter in the West. A man has to be careful about what he eats and his observances, true. But what about a woman? Think of it. The way an orthodox woman wants to dress—and I was a very orthodox woman—the way you want to dress, interact, meet, or not meet other people, live, all of it is under constant assault by ordinary life in the West. That crazy woman on the bus was not such an exception, after all. She just expressed without any inhibition what so many others think politely.

It builds up a core of bitterness in you. On the one hand, you cannot really be part of everything that might empower you as a person, give you the options you want;

you do not want to part of all this, the parties, the flirting, the option to grab a sandwich without checking whether it is pork or beef, halal or not, the simple ability to walk down a street without feeling like you are an alien from Mars, and sometimes being treated like one! You opt out of the glitter of the West, because of your belief. It takes strength to do so. More strength than Muslim men realise: I wonder if imams would insist on the hijab as much as they do, if they had to put it on themselves and cope with the consequences in ordinary life. It takes strength and character. You know that, and yet you are told by every stupid politician or journalist, every white man who, as far as thinking is concerned, has never done anything that was not done by the very first white monkey-Adam in his family, every such idiot can tell you, will tell you, implicitly or explicitly, that you are an automaton, that you are brainwashed or daft.

And there are people on the left, yes, people like you, who defend women like the woman I used to be, but pityingly, as one would fight for the rights of a performing seal in a circus. You cannot imagine the bitterness all of this builds up in our souls. Sometimes, I would do anything to be free of all this, to be myself without being considered a monster or a curiosity. And what Hejjiye and others were telling us about the newly created Islamic State, it seemed to be that sort of place, a country where I thought I could be myself.

I won't deny I had other reasons too. Ammi was putting pressure on me to finalize the marriage proposal. I was frustrated at the dead end my life had reached, with none of my applications working out sufficiently for me to be able to act on them. There was this desire, oh, how strong it had been, inculcated in me throughout my life, differently in my parents' small flat and among my friends who wore jilbabs and niqabs, and differently again in our mosque and on the Internet, this desire, as Ameena wished, too, the longing to simply live a life that was meaningful and just, based on the *sira*, the life of Prophet Mohammad. And, no doubt, Ameena and I had talked each other into a situation where each sustained the other, both prevented the other from expressing any real doubt about the justness of the cause or our interpretation of our faith. And yet, it took time before I told Ameena that I would join her.

***

"Just leave. Just pack your bags and leave," Hejjiye would often tell us, when we complained about the roadblocks erected by ordinary life in our pursuit of the *Sunnah* way. "You are a big girl now. No one can stop you."

I always took it for a rhetorical statement. But then, one day, suddenly it struck me: I was an adult, I had money in my bank, I had a passport, I was no longer living with my Ammi or brother. *Yes,* I thought, *I am a big girl.*

I could pack my bags and leave.

***

The rest of it was surprisingly simple. We knew that we would be in Istanbul before anyone even started suspecting that we were gone. But we did not take any risks, or, rather, Ameena did not. We tried to act like two young girls visiting Istanbul. Both Hejjiye and Hassan had insisted on that. We knew that there were other girls like us, leaving Western nations to join the jihad. But we were still in an early wave; the Western media had yet to make a few dozen women in each country sound like there was a veritable exodus, as if all Muslim women in Europe were about to jump on planes to Istanbul. Security was not too tight yet. And we had received exact instructions. Leaving the airport, we took the metro to Bayrampaşa, a suburban district of Istanbul on the European side of the city. We were supposed to wait at the main bus stop there, and we would be contacted by two or three men.

How would they know us? *They would.* How would we know them? *They would refer to Hejjiye.* What if something goes wrong? *It won't. You have to trust us. Have faith. Allah will be with you. Allah is with us.*

Hejjiye was always big on trust.

There was a hot-air balloon against the whitish-blue sky at a distance. Ameena put her camera away. She wanted to discard it, but we decided that might attract needless attention.

No men approached us. It started getting dark. Buses were being announced and they were leaving. Passengers passed us regularly. One woman even came up to us and said something. She must have asked if we needed help. We did not understand her, but indicated to her that we were OK. She went away.

Then, suddenly, they were there, next to us. Two young men and an old one. "Hejjiye send," said one of the younger men, who was the only one to speak English. Without a word more, they picked up our bags and walked us to a bus that was about to leave. The old man got in with us; the young man who spoke English said, "He has you tickets. He take you." Then the two young men left, fading into the crowd as silently as they had appeared.

The old man had a thin, severe face. His beard was

almost white, but he could not have been older than sixty. Even though we were both fully veiled now, showing only our eyes, he did not look at us even once. We might as well have been travelling separately.

I must have fallen asleep. When I woke up it was dark and we were in the countryside: there were only distant lights, as if in a hamlet across fields. It seemed to be a slightly hilly region. The headlights of the bus often fell on trees that seemed to be oak, and indeed, when I woke up, in that thin no-man's land between sleep and wakefulness I thought, because of the oaks, I suppose, that I was on a bus going through some part of England. Then full consciousness sank in, and I realised— probably for the first time—the immensity of my act. I had left behind everything I knew, all the people I had known, for a new life. Strangely, when I thought of all the people I had left behind, at that time I thought first of James and only then of my Ammi, Mohammad and the others. It was strange to think of any of them, and even more so James, in that alien darkness, occasionally pierced by a light from some hamlet.

Ameena was sleeping next to me. The old man sat behind us and, somehow, without having to look back, I knew he was wide awake, staring impassively into the darkness.

An hour later some low buildings appeared and the bus pulled up at a stop. The old man indicated to us to get out. Some other passengers exited the bus and were met by relatives at the stop. The bus drove on after a short halt. No one had met us. But that seemed to be in order. The old man nodded at the road, pointing in a particular direction. We obeyed his mute instructions.

The old man walked briskly, carrying two of our bags with ease. He walked us to a small house down a narrow alley, not far from the bus stop, and indicated to us to take our bags and go in. It was dark inside. When our eyes got used to the murk, we realised that there were six women in the room. One of them spoke English. We were going to cross the border with these women and the old man who waited outside. They were introduced to us, after the woman who was speaking to us congratulated Ameena and me for taking the right decision and joining the jihad, for Allah would surely bless us in this life and the next. It appeared that four of the women, including the speaker, were of different nationalities, mostly crossing the border to join their husbands. The other two were Turkish: the older sister was married to a jihadi, who was accompanying her back to his "posting," and the younger sister, Halide, would be joining Hejjiye with us. Like us, Halide had finally chosen the way of the faith and the righteous, God bless her and make her prosper. Halide smiled shyly at us, blinking behind her glasses, and said hesitatingly, "Some English … I speak a little." She looked much younger than us, but it turned out that we were just a year older than her.

It was then that we discovered that Hejjiye ran an orphanage and home for women in a town on the Syria-Iraq border. We would be helping her run the institution. In Ameena's case, of course, it would be only for a few weeks, until Hassan could come over and marry her. As for me, the Arab woman continued, why, I was such a beauty, I would get a hundred suitors in a week! I laughed at the notion, which disconcerted the speaker a bit, but then she attributed it to legitimate shyness and patted my head, as if I was a favourite pet. It surprised me that the women in the room seemed to know everything about us; as if we were not just two girls recently out of school, seeking a life that made sense; as if we were some great achievement on the part of the jihadis, a victory of sorts, an endorsement.

Us?

***

It must have been easier to cross over around that time; Turkey had not yet been put in the spotlight for not stopping jihadis and their families from entering Syria. We went the very next evening by road. The old man did not go with us. Instead two middle-aged men—one of them married to a woman with us, and the other a relative of some sort too—drove us in a battered Peugeot station wagon. As always, we were part of a small caravan. There were two families in two smaller cars with us. The women were all fully veiled now, and Ameena and I had been instructed to stay behind the other women and not to speak in the presence of anyone else. On the event, we were not interrogated; I doubt we took any of the main roads for long. As we got closer to the border, we often turned onto side roads and country paths. Sometimes we stopped for hours, as the men went out and spoke on their mobiles. I don't think there was even a checkpoint where we crossed from Turkey to Syria.

But there was an alarm less than an hour after we set off. We had stopped at dusk to enable the men to say their prayers; women had to do so sitting in one place inside the vehicles. It was the hour when dust mingles with dusk, so that the darkness seems riven and deceptive, as if it was smoke rising off the earth. Even though it was too dark now to see far into the distance, I could make out the silhouette of a barren hill—probably brown, with clumps of bushes, in keeping with the region we had passed through—on one side of the road, about a kilometre away. There appeared to be a large spare building or an old fort on its peak. A small path—unpaved—joined the road from that direction. Around us was largely plain land, with grass and thin trees. The men had spread their rugs on the grass to pray.

Suddenly, in a swirl of dust, sound and yellow headlights, two jeeps came roaring down the path that descended from the hill. Before the men managed to get back to our cars, the jeeps had blocked the road on both sides. Armed men—in some sort of uniform—jumped out. There was a lot of shouting and gesturing, on both sides, and then one of our men came around to us and asked us to contribute money. We gave him much of the cash we had. We had more than the other women. The man wrapped it all up in a handkerchief and handed the bundle to one of the armed men. Then, as suddenly as they had descended on the road, the jeeps roared away, back into the darkness of the hill or the fort.

When the men who were driving our vehicle returned and started the station wagon, they were laughing. They said something in Turkish, and the women with us laughed too. Halide translated for Ameena and me: "He say, how do you say it, he say that devil is good at corrupting his own people, which is good for party of Allah."

The men laughed again.

***

We had been crammed into the station wagon, but the drive was not unpleasant—almost as if we were a family returning from a picnic. Once we skirted a river that, we were told, was the Euphrates, or maybe a branch of it. I glimpsed a dark waterwheel. The others mentioned the Euphrates dismissingly, but the name had a historic ring in our ears. We were trying not to speak English to one another too often—partly to practise our Arabic and partly not to seem supercilious in that company—but I could not help saying to Ameena, "Allah, it is really t'Euphrates! A thought it existed only in me textbooks!" I was so excited that I slipped into dialect!

After crossing into Syria, or maybe a bit earlier, the landscape got even flatter. There were no more oak trees. The land felt drier too. But, in the morning, as we woke up in the back of the station wagon, there were pistachio trees and stretches of wild grain. Once we passed through a grove of rose plums and the men stopped to look for some, but it was too early or too late in the season.

Syria had been announced to us, but we would have deduced as much on our own. A few minutes after we were told that we had entered Syria—there had been no border post—I saw my first bombed building, its girders reaching out like arms into the sky. It was only after we had crossed into Syria, as we approached the town of Raqqa, that we were stopped and interrogated. Ameena and I were asked to show our passports. But this was a checkpoint run by the Daesh, or their allies, and we were let into Raqqa without any problem.

Raqqa was a devastated city; that is what I recall. Remember, this was much before the real carpet-bombing by Syrian government forces—which commenced only in November. But it was a ravaged place even in August.

It is one thing to see images of buildings devastated by war; it is another thing to see them in person. The twisted girders, the blasted walls, the houses pockmarked with bullet holes, the fallen beams and bricks, the craters blasted here and there—they all strike you as greatly unjust, hugely un-natural when you first see them. There seems to be something wrong about such gross disregard for human achievement and hopes. We were not prepared for this. And yet, in a few days, we got used to such scenes of devastation.

We did not stay long in Raqqa. All the women got off except Halide, Ameena, and I. We were to be driven to Hejjiye's town by three other men, this time dressed in the Daesh way—military fatigues, black balaclavas—and fully armed, who had been waiting for us and were quite impatient to be gone. A small caravan of three cars and a lorry—the cars full of women and children, and the lorry of goods for some markets—had been waiting for us. But it was too late to leave now. We were put up in a house where the women treated us like heroines. For the first time in two days, we had good warm food. Because Ameena and I were taken to be from Pakistan—though I had visited that country only a couple of times as a kid and neither Ameena nor her parents had ever been there—the family made something called Kebab Hindi. It was supposed to be, as "Hindi" suggested, an Indian concoction, but we had never had a kebab like it: it was not the spices they had put in the kebab, which were similar to the spices my Ammi would have used, but their use of capsicum and pomegranate mo-lasses. No, it was not something—I am sure—you would get in India or Pakistan. But it was delicious. Or perhaps we were hungry and tired. We fell asleep—now used to sharing beds with other women—almost immediately after dinner. I slept fitfully, my dreams a shifting collage of memories from home, memories I tried to push as far away as I could when awake. At dawn, after the first prayers, we left.

A NEW LIFE

Let me call Hejjiye's town just the Town. That should suffice. Let it stand in for all such towns in those parts. That is apt, isn't it? All those towns where one part of a building aspires toward urbanity in the way a wall is shaped or an archway structured—the precision, intention, accomplishment of it—while the rest of the building fails, is overlooked, gets reduced to something that seems tacked on in a rush. All those towns where the traffic outstrips the width of the roads. All those towns where you can find brands from New York and Paris if you only know which dark, untidy shop to go to. And now, at least in that part of the world, all those towns where entire streets resemble the face of a demented old man, grinning, dark gaps between his teeth, his skin discoloured and riven. Why isolate this town for attention when it was no different from a thousand other towns around it?

The drive after Raqqa had taken three days, as we had stopped for the nights with families, and joined a number of different caravans. The men driving us had changed too, and we had been provided with papers to explain our strange circumstances—we were travelling without male family members. Joining the caravans might have been required because of that, too.

The further we drove, the more arid the land got. Soon after Raqqa, we were driving through flatlands that I thought were like the steppes. There were some sheep but not much for them to graze on. The oak and rose plum trees had disappeared. Occasionally I saw white wormwood—shrubs that were like explosions of grey-green dust in the landscape, grenades of chlorophyll tossed into the semidesert, their fuzzy foliage reflecting the sunlight. But that was it.

Then the town. Or the Town. The two cars with us in that final caravan stopped there, near a stone building, half bombed down and half boarded up, that, we were told, had been the souk; our Ford drove on. The souk was the only really old building that I saw in the Town. What was the Town like, you ask? It must have been bigger once. It must have contained more people until recently. That, I could tell immediately: the broken buildings, the way people looked at us, the dust-covered skeletons of cars by the roadside. Not far from the souk, there was a modern-looking marketplace, all concrete and bricks: two shops were gutted, a few were shuttered. But at least a dozen shops were still open. One of them was an electronics shop. There was a clothes and footwear shop with its glass front intact, except for a single bullet hole. I spotted posters of Nike and other such brands—though the sections of the posters that must have displayed pictures of women had been ripped away. Some elderly women were haggling around a table of vegetables and poultry at a corner of the market square. Two old men, wearing traditional dress, sat on a bench under a tree next to a boarded-up shop, pulling on a hookah. I did not see a single young man or woman out in the streets, apart from soldiers dressed in the Daesh way—the military fatigues, black scarves, and dark caps or balaclavas making them stand out like a hawk does in blue skies of the desert.

Then we took a couple of turns and we had suddenly left the Town behind us.

About a kilometre ahead of us, across fields that might have been cultivated once, there rose what was unarguably the most impressive building in the Town. This is Hejjiye's orphanage, the men driving us said.

***

Looking back, I wonder why I found the orphanage building so impressive at that moment, as we drove up to it. The building was only one-storeyed; it was simply whitewashed, with dark splotches showing here and there. But it covered a large area, shaped like a flattened U. One of the flanks of the U, I discovered later, held dormitories for students. Some of them were no longer being used. This flank could be locked up; a metal grille separated it from the rest of the building. The other flank contained separate rooms—rooms for teachers, a kitchen, and some storerooms. At the very end of the teachers' flank there was a room with bars on it, a room with its own toilet; I did not understand the function of this room until much later. There were common toilets in both the wings. As the flanks had rooms on both sides, basically you felt as if you were entering a tunnel. The middle section contained our classrooms and Hejjiye's office. This was different—open on one side, though fenced in with metal grilles. You entered the building through a massive door in this section. There were doors at the back of the building, too, letting out onto a dusty football field, about five hundred metres beyond which lay ruins of a series of houses that, I was told, had once belonged to Shia families. But the doors leading to this football field from the classrooms were now boarded up and locked. The only way into the building was through the large door opposite Hejjiye's office, right in the centre of the U. But as if that was not enough, there was a wall closing the opening of the U, too, with a huge metal gate in front of it. The courtyard this walled U created was large enough to park a few lorries, if required. In one corner there was even a well with a pump to draw water from. Some shrubs and an olive tree, square and short, with dusty green leaves, grew around the well. The tree had sparrows nesting in it, and sometimes a flock of pigeons would settle in the courtyard.

Driving up to this building from the town side, what we noticed first was the wall closing the mouth of the U and the huge gate. The wall was decorated with beautiful ceramic tiles, mostly in some shade of blue. They looked old. The gate was of wrought iron, with a smaller door embedded in it. Sheets of metal had been welded onto the gate, so you could no longer look inside the U. Still, the place appeared beautiful to my eyes, and it was only later that I realised why: it was the only undamaged building I had seen for miles now. It did not even have bullet holes. The war had passed it by.

We were dropped off by the gate. There were two small guardhouses on both sides on the outside; inside were Daesh guards, but dressed like locals. They were not flying a flag. It was obvious that they did not want to attract attention to the orphanage. One of the guards called Hejjiye on a mobile, and the door embedded in the gate was opened from inside. The men driving us wished the peace of Allah on us and drove off.

We entered through the gate.

***

A small occasion had been organised for us by Hejjiye. But it was almost sunset, and Hejjiye postponed the celebration to after the Maghrib prayer. She instructed us to get washed first and showed us to our rooms in the teachers' flank. The teachers and chaperones—and, increasingly, wives or mothers of jihadis who had nowhere else to go—slept in the rooms, usually three or four persons per room. Ameena and I were given a two-bed room. I realised this was a favour to us.

After the Maghrib prayer, we had our small celebration, in which Hejjiye welcomed us: she introduced Halide too, but mostly she spoke of me and Ameena. She stressed that we were among tens of thousands of true Muslims who, captive in the West, were now yearning to join the jihad. "They are on their way, these brothers and sisters, as you can see, children," Hejjiye said, addressing the orphans. "They are on their way, and our ranks will swell, until the flood of faith will wash away the sins and atrocities of America and its allies! Surely, this will be! Surely, it is predicted!"

The girls responded with "amin" and "alhamdulillah." Later we had a small party, good coffee, which had started getting difficult to obtain even then, some dates, and Turkish sweets. Hejjiye left with a couple of other women, who lived with their husbands in town, and the girls crowded around Ameena and me, touching us shyly, as if to convince themselves that we were real, until the other teachers and chaperones shooed them away.

But I put one question to Hejjiye—I had been burning to ask her from the moment I had arrived!—before she left for the night. "Where is Batala?" I asked her. She looked surprised; she did not seem to understand me. When she finally understood, she laughed. "Ah, my little cat," she said. "Those were photos from almost two years ago. Batala disappeared last summer. Never came back one night." She looked thoughtful for a moment. "Lots of pets have been killed or maimed. Firing, bombs, mines, booby traps. And then, to be honest, who has time for pets now?"

***

Travelling had left us fatigued, and I had been able to sleep most nights from sheer tiredness. But, as we settled into Hejjiye's orphanage, I was made conscious of the difference of this life that I had chosen and the life I had led in England. I had assumed that a shared faith would be enough to bridge the gap, and now, for the first time, I felt unsure. The beds, for instance. I could hardly fall asleep on them—they were so hard and narrow. It took me three or four nights to get used to them.

Strangely, Ameena managed to sleep easily on them. From the first night. She just turned around and slipped into a deep slumber, while I tossed and turned on my bunk almost until dawn. When I asked her about it, she said, "Your parents never let yer go camping, did they?" No, they didn't. My father could not have dreamt of letting his daughter spend a night with strangers, especially strangers that included boys and male teachers. "See," Ameena laughed, "After all, there are some advantages to a non-halal upbringing."

But I won't bother you with such details. I could tell you much more about myself: small things, like my difficulty in getting used to life without toilet paper, despite growing up in a family that was, shall we say, ambidextrous in this regard. Or bigger things, like the girl who would, for no reason at all, lie down suddenly and pretend to be dead—I almost panicked the first time I witnessed it, but the other girls were used to it and would, despite Hejjiye discouraging it, outline her in chalk and step around her until, an hour or two later, she would get up, dust herself and walk off as if nothing had happened. But no, I do not want to talk too much about these things; I want to tell you about Ameena, mostly.

***

As Ameena and I were introduced to our duties and routines, by Hejjiye, we realised that in real life this handsome, decisive woman, with a broad face and strong eyebrows, was not that different from her Internet persona: something of a mother and a matron, a professor and a preacher, a confessor and a boss. She did not live in the orphanage, but she obviously had the highest authority among the women there. (I never saw her husband, the Town's Daesh commander, though it was said that he would sometimes drive Hejjiye to the orphanage and pick her up. If he was one of the men who entered our courtyard on a rare occasion, usually for a preachy lecture, no one pointed him out to me. He was more of a rumour to us, known by his nom-de-guerre of Abu Jalal.)

Hejjiye would arrive at ten, almost on the dot, unless detained by some emergency, and leave a bit after dark. She was always driven to the place and picked up by the Daesh, accompanied by other women from town. We knew that she lived in a house in town where her husband sometimes spent the nights. Like all other women, she never ventured alone out of home; she would be accompanied by at least one of her husband's other three wives, sometimes all three of them. But she was the oldest of the lot, and in any case, they behaved more like her little sisters than co-wives. She could tell them what to do, and they would execute her commands with absolute obedience. No wonder, the thought crossed my mind, that Hejjiye was so happy about the institution of polygamy, something I had accepted as part of my faith but never really had to face up to until then: her husband's three wives were the perfect combination of sister and slave to her. I wondered what her co-wives thought of the institution. But I pushed the thought away from my mind: after all, Islam did sanction four wives, though my parents had insisted that it was only on the condition that all four were treated equally, and I found that hard to imagine in the case of Hejjiye. It was difficult to imagine any woman being treated equally around her: she was a strikingly hand-some woman, taller than any of us, broad in the shoulders, but with feminine proportions, always in good humour—as if she was a model in a TV competition—and never with even a shadow of doubt on her face.

It turned out that, apart from Hejjiye, Halide was the only other teacher who had conversational English. I was growing quite fond of Halide, who also took to eating with Ameena and me: we ate in groups of six or seven, seated around a large plate, usually heaped with rice, around which there would be meat and vegetables. Gravy or, in the begin-ning, before it got scarcer, butter, would be poured on the rice, and we would all dig in. It took some getting used to: Ameena and I had grown up with knowledge of commu-nal eating in Islam, but had not practised it—even during our journey the families that had hosted us had handed us plates and spoons. Halide would also join us during our spare moments. Not that the routine Hejjiye had devised and imposed left anyone with much spare time. Think of soldiers living in barracks and turn it into a female version, shorn of anything that only a man could do: that will give you an idea of how full our days were, how regimented. A lazy mind is the Devil's workshop, Hejjiye would say.

Yes, well, if you insist, I will take another cup of coffee. Did I tell you that despite all the Islamic sisterhood on display in Hejjiye's orphanage, we were divided into groups that bickered over how to brew our coffee and tea? We never agreed on just one way to make coffee or tea.

***

Ameena did not like Hejjiye too much in person. She had been happier with her on the Internet. "A didn't come all t'way 'ere just to get me 'nother mam," she whispered to me just a few days after we got there. Hejjiye, too, grew progressively cold toward Ameena after the first meeting; she was much friendlier with me. I think when Ameena got married, about a month after her arrival, it afforded mutual relief to both Hejjiye and Ameena. Also to me (though I missed Ameena after she left) because I could feel the tension between them, and I was afraid that Ameena would have an outburst one day soon. Ameena, I realised then, found mother figures more unpalatable than father figures. I had enough understanding of people and the situation to realise that Hejjiye was not someone you could offend openly. Luckily, Ameena got married before their growing antagonism came to a head.

But this was more than a month after we arrived at the orphanage. Hassan was some sort of a deputy commander in a large village on the other side of the Iraqi border, and he could not find time or get leave—I do not remember which—to come to the Town. He stayed in touch with Ameena on the Internet, though.

Actually, the first thing we did after settling down in the orphanage was to ask Hejjiye about Internet facilities. Almost as if we were checking into a hotel in Europe! We had switched off our mobiles and not even tried to go online from the moment we left our flat for London. Hejjiye had insisted on that. But, despite pretending to each other that we did not care, we could not help wondering how our families and friends had taken to our disappearance.

Hejjiye informed us that the orphanage did not have Wi-Fi. But there was an Internet room, used occasionally by the students, though only under supervision. We could dock our laptops there. Teachers and chaperones were allowed to access the room anytime they wished to do so, but students were locked into their wing—two chaperones with them—every night. This, Hejjiye said, was for their own safety.

Reception was poor in the Internet room. But we spent a few nights checking on news from home. This was before those British schoolgirls ... what were their names? One of them was almost Ameena's namesake—Amira, I think she was called. You know the case? Well, yes, that's good; it was before those three fled to join the jihad and the matter became a media highlight. Our disappearance had not been highlighted that much. There was almost nothing from Mohammad, except for an appeal asking me to return. Ammi had not spoken to anyone, which was not surprising, given her rudimentary English. There were a couple of interviews with Ameena's mum and one with her father, in which they expressed surprise at Ameena's "radicalisation."

I could tell they were torn between their concern for their daughter and their need to stress that they were by no means fundamentalist Muslims. Ameena's father blamed Western intelligence agencies for failing to do their job, and Aunty insinuated that I had "brainwashed" her. There was an article, I think in the *Daily Mirror*, where some of our ex-classmates had been interviewed: it carried a photo of Alex, looking even more handsome now, who was described as the ex-boyfriend of Ameena. Next to Alex's shot, there was a photo of me, labelled with Ameena's name. But apart from that, there was very little about our disappearance—and nothing much would come out in the future, either, except some more bitter remarks about me from Aunty.

We had closed or discontinued our old e-mail, Twitter, and Facebook accounts before leaving, only retaining the jihadi personas that we had created recently. It was the best way, Hejjiye had told us months ago, to prevent family and friends from blackmailing you emotionally. I recall a line from her, for like so many Islamists from the West, she liked quoting from the Bible to "prove" that the Quran was its "uncorrupted" version: "Remember, Jesus, even according to that censored, truncated once-holy book, the Bible, had asked his followers to give up their families in order to follow him. There can be nothing greater than God!"

Our jihadi persona pages were bursting with hits. Here, the story was different: between us, we had made at least a thousand new "friends" and "followers" in the past few days. Over the next few weeks, the numbers grew; I stopped checking months ago, and for all I know, the numbers are still growing! If we felt some doubt about our decision back then, the outpouring of sympathy and praise from these anonymous supporters—from Yemen and Egypt, from India and Pakistan, from Canada and Denmark—helped us overcome it.

You've read articles about how the Internet has created a lonelier world, with people isolating themselves behind their screens, connecting to a flat keyboard rather than in a park or at a party. Yes and no. Yes and no. It depends on who you are, and where. Some of us never had parks or parties to connect in. Some of us never will.

***

Hejjiye might not have taken to Ameena, but she did like the notion of marrying her to a jihadi. I realised later that this was probably Hejjiye's favourite hobby: she loved arranging marriages for her girls, and for any teacher who might show the inclination. In some ways, you might say, her orphanage was an Islamic marriage bureau for the jihadis.

Despite Hejjiye's enthusiasm when news came that Hassan was on his way to us, the wedding itself was a plain affair. If Ammi was slightly disappointed by Mohammad's wedding, which had reduced all the cultural paraphernalia of her kasbah marriages to a bare minimum, she would have been scandalised beyond words at Ameena's wedding. There could be no music, of course; there had been no music at Mohammad's wedding either. But there had been a couple of ritual ceremonies where the women had chanted a song or two, badly out of tune after decades of life and English in England.

There was no question of even such half-hearted ceremonies here. We hardly had a function. Hassan and the men who came with him were in a hurry. They stopped in one of the guardhouses outside. We could only hear them. Hassan sounded like what he was: an officer on duty. The mullah hustled back and forth through the door in the gate, got the signatures of the bride and the bridegroom and the necessary number of witnesses on both sides, and declared them married, without any further ado or talk. There was a hurried meal, the men and women eating separately, divided by that huge metal gate, instead of the usual flimsy partition, and then Ameena was gone, with a brave smile at me. She and Hassan were going to stay in a hotel in town for two or three days and then head back to Hassan's posting.

I think it was a brave smile.

***

With Ameena gone, our life settled into a routine. I heard good things about her as a wife from Hejjiye; I assumed that the Chinese packet of artificial hymens must have worked. That was a greater relief than I have indicated to you. I had been worried about the ability of a made-in-China hymen to deceive a jihadi. But Ameena wasn't, at least not in London, which was the last time we had spoken of it. Men, she had assured me, are alike: they know very little about women and believe what they want to. Ameena in those days still had what I can only call chutzpah. She had shared that with Alex. Maybe that too had drawn him to her in those mad weeks years ago, which, I feared, had marked her for good. As for me, yes, I worried. But did I condemn her in the depths of my soul? To be honest, I have never been the condemning sort, despite the intensity of my faith. In those days I was obsessed with rights and wrongs—my Islam was still a minefield of rights and wrongs—but I left condemnation to others, to imams, to men, to Allah. So, no, I did not condemn Ameena. I was very worried for her. I knew what would happen if her subterfuge was discovered. I breathed a sigh of relief only after her honeymoon.

Ameena called three or four times in the initial month or two, once from the Town itself, after her first night, and at least a couple of times after reaching her new home: each time she chirped happily on the phone, like any newlywed girl. Then she just texted and e-mailed, but less and less often. I thought I recognised the pattern: don't all newlyweds go through a phase when they lose touch with their old friends?

I was busy enough. We were in a relatively safe area of the region. When bombs fell or guns were fired, they sounded far away from us. I think Daesh had selected the orphanage on purpose; parts of it had been built as a madrassa two or three centuries ago, or perhaps earlier. Such historical dates existed in a blur for Hejjiye and us. The madrassa had been abandoned. But in modern times, it had been restored and expanded into a school for girls, with an orphanage attached to it. Known as the only institution of the sort in those parts, it had escaped the civil war because of its reputation. The various sides had not fought their battles in or around it, though the Shia houses behind it had been attacked and destroyed by the victorious Daesh. The orphanage still seemed to be functioning. At least, that is the impression I had. About two dozen orphans—some of them young women—lived in the student dormitories on one side of the building.

Mostly, between fixed half-hour breaks for prayers and meals, the girls were taught the Quran and the hadith and some Daesh-sanctioned commentaries on them. There was also a class, usually run by Hejjiye, but other foreign teachers—I was one of them—were asked to contribute on some days: this was a class on news, which ranged from celebrations of Daesh victories to condemnation of Western propaganda. Hejjiye would regularly surf for news that could be used, and I was given that job too, once I won her trust with my much-praised "humility" and "meekness." A couple of other teachers surfed for news in other languages. Whenever we found anything that we thought revealed the duplicity of Western forces, we brought it to Hejjiye's notice; she decided whether or not it could be used. The news ranged from standard stuff, like civilians being killed by American or coalition forces in Afghanistan or reports of Muslim insurgency in China or Kashmir, to more obscure articles, such as news of high levels of uranium being detected in the urine of Afghan villagers as a consequence of weapons employed by the Americans.

I still have hundreds of such news items jumbled up in my head, and I cannot really make up my mind about some of them: it was difficult to distinguish between truth and propaganda before I joined the jihadis, and it became—as I realised later—even more difficult to do so when I was with them. I cannot say that the difficulty has disappeared; I fear that there are too many official liars on all sides. But let me not talk about what I think now; I should stick to my story. The stress was on religious studies—the Quran and the hadith, with commentaries, which got sparser as (I realise now) more and more Islamic schools of theology came out and criticised Daesh. But there were also regular talks about current issues—with the focus on the "plight of Muslims" in the "lands of war," by which Hejjiye meant almost all lands outside the Islamic State, because Daesh did not consider most Muslims, let alone non-Muslims, as practicing the right faith.

I must say that initially I was impressed by what they were trying to do. It confirmed my suspicion that the Western media had exaggerated the villainy of Daesh. We were being told about how they had banned math and literature and whatnot, and it is true that these subjects were not taught at the orphanage. Not that I found it problematic then. I told myself that these were very orthodox people—more orthodox even than my father or brother—and they had objections to such "Western" subjects. But, unlike what the papers had said in England, these people did seem to want to help women and learn at least a bit about the world. Why else would they run an orphanage like this?

There wasn't much of a town life, the way you would understand it. In any case, we could not go out on our own, even in groups. But in the initial months, I did not miss all that. I found it a relief to be with women, or—in the case of the odd guest imam—with men whose interest in you was regulated by religion. I found it a relief to go out, on the occasions when we did, in a group of women (escorted by some male relative of one of the women), and not to be pierced by the occasional look of surprise or even dislike that my attire would elicit in England.

There was a purposeful order to my life that had been lacking earlier. It helped me resist those moments, usually early in the morning and late at night, when I kept thinking of what my mother might be doing in our old flat: especially at night, because we were two hours ahead of England, and when I was lying in bed, trying to sleep, Ammi would be tidying up in the flat, cleaning her precious little scullery, rinsing the bigger utensils, stacking the dishwasher, or saying her prayers. Lying in bed, I would yearn to be able to see her just once more, to be able to tell her that all was well with me—and I could have called her, but I knew it would be even more selfish of me. It would just create problems for her back home. For my brother Mohammad too. I told myself—I tell myself even today—that it was best for me to stay away from her life, once I had abandoned it. No doctor can cure the past, as James might have said back in school. ("Kwacken," he would actually say, not "cure.") I could not have looked after her; my brother would have done so, anyway; I was just meant to be married off to a stranger. Sometime when I was twelve or thirteen—perhaps soon after my big sulk on being forced to return the kitten—I had drifted away from her. Our conversations—we used to lie in bed talking nonsense (*Gup-shup*, Ammi called it)—had diminished as I entered my teens and my interests no longer meshed with her experience. I suppose this happens to all mothers and daughters. But it was worse in our case. My mother did not even speak—no more than some laboured sentences—that language, English, which was inevitably my first language. Not my mother tongue, you might say, but definitely my first language. Even her religion was different from mine, I realise now. There was love between us, but very little to express and even less to share.

But there was unspeakable love between us, and now I missed my Ammi not in the larger things of life—no, we had not really shared those once I grew older—but in the smaller ones. For instance, her habit of waking up before all of us, saying her prayers, and brewing tea—which would be waiting for us, with a plate of arrowroot biscuits, when we finished our prayers. It was these small things, which I had taken for granted and had not missed even after moving to Ameena's flat, that started haunting me now. I tell you, I was grateful for the stark routines of Hejjiye's orphanage.

We would get up at dawn, with the first call to prayer, which was followed by compulsory reading from the Quran for an hour. Then the different groups of students, each headed by a "teacher," would take care of various domestic duties: cleaning up, laundry, cooking, and so on. Each group had its chores for the week fixed every Friday by Hejjiye and her aides. After an early breakfast, the classes and lectures started, punctuated throughout the day by the required prayers. They ended with the namaz at sunset. That is when Hejjiye left, with a couple of others who lived, like her, elsewhere in the town, and we were left with some free time after dinner had been cooked and consumed. That was, with minor differences, our daily routine, except on Friday. Fridays were holidays, but that simply meant fewer classes. We still had chores to do, though. Friday was the day when we could sit out in the courtyard for an hour or so between prayers, and scatter grain or crumbs to the pigeons and sparrows.

I was happy we had such a full schedule—prayer, duty, teaching, more prayer, studying, meal, Quran readings, a series of small sombre events, all of them following one another, with hardly a pause in between—until we were almost ready to go to bed. I was thankful for such extreme busyness in this isolated, almost self-contained building. It was the only thing that prevented me from thinking too much about my family, especially about my mother. Mohammad and Bhabhi I could recall without a massive pang of regret—I had realised that in some ways they allowed me to go, even encouraged me to drift out of their lives and, whether they did so consciously or not, my parents' flat. I knew Islam. I knew I was entitled to a share of the flat. Mohammad knew it too. But it had never been brought up by him or Bhabhi. A small part of my mind gnawed my heart with resentment over such matters, and I hastily put the salve of "Allah's will" on it. But the gnawing turned that corner of my heart into a calloused disinterest in my big brother—whom I had adored, once upon a time—and his life. My Ammi was different. There was very little to share between me and my mother, I have told you. True. In England. But things changed in Syria; they changed slowly. I did not feel I gained more to share with her—no, there was even less to share now, for my life had taken a turn that was as alien to her upbringing and experience as England had been—but I understood her better. The longer I stayed in the orphanage, the more I felt that I understood her. I understood her better here, in this bleak, desert-like place than I had in England. I was relieved to drown myself in chores.

***

Any kind of celebration—even any display of happiness or joy—on the Prophet's birthday was considered *bid'ah,* a heretical innovation, among us at the orphanage. Back home, we had observed the Prophet's birthday with a small *milaad,* but even that was not permitted by Hejjiye. All we could do on that day was read from the Quran or offer extra prayers. But this was by no means the only festival that disappeared.

I had *not* grown up in a family that celebrated festivals in what you might call a "cultural" manner. With a few token exceptions for the sake of my Ammi, we had observed festivals in a kind of bare and denuded style. (Salafist, you say? Well, maybe, if you want to give it a tag.) I remember that, as a child, when we had gone to an Eid Milan in London—organised by a distant branch of my father's family that had grown up in Karachi and moved to London in the previous generation—I had been dazzled by the party. It had its quota of speckled beards, hennaed hair, and bloated bellies, which was what I associated with Eid Milans. But these were in the minority and relegated to a frowning corner, where my father, despite being thin, black-bearded, and openly balding, joined them. The rest of the guests? "Ooh la la!" as Ameena would say in school. We used to wear new clothes for Eid, but what was on display at that London party was beyond anything I had seen: it was like a scene from a Bollywood film, women decked in glittering bangles and necklaces, with exquisite coiffures. The hall—it had been arranged in a hotel's banquet room—was lavishly decked with flowers. There had been choice Pakistani and British dishes, all halal of course, but not all familiar to me: chicken tandoori, pulao, lamb roganjosh, rasmalai, and more on one side and pies, oak-smoked salmon, and a wedding cake on the other. Then, in the evening, there had been a show by a ghazal singer. It was when the musicians were tuning their instruments on a small stage in the hall that my father made his excuses and herded us out. On the way back home, in his cab, he was scathing in his dismissal of the party and the family: "These are the types that have an Eid luncheon at the Sind Club or Boat Club or Gymkhana in Karachi. Their brats will do get-togethers—GTs they call it, GTs, the ETs!—which are just like any regular party, including drinking like the whites, or go to Thailand or Dubai on vacation instead. The best of both worlds, they will tell you!

Well, there is a world after this world, too, and Allah will decide who gets the best of that world." I was six or seven, and bedazzled by the party and the people: listening to my father's acrid remarks during the drive back, I felt ashamed of my own enjoyment of the party, and thereafter I remained wary of all such glitter.

So yes, my Islam was by no means like the Islam of that class. My Islam did not permit "GTs" for Eid because we had no wish to become ETs! But despite this, I must have realised quite early on that Hejjiye's Islam was narrower and darker, like the wings on both sides of her orphanage. There were fewer festivals in Hejjiye's Islam; even the ones we did celebrate were bleaker. Initially, this made me feel confirmed in my decisions: after all, this is what I had been seeking in England, a space to practise nothing but my faith.

It was not just the festivals that had diminished; the world had shrunk too. To begin with, there were two or three group trips to the weekly market, under the supervision of Hejjiye and male members of her family or the family of one of her chaperones, but these stopped very soon after we arrived, with Daesh clamping down even further on the movement of women. Sometimes we still had visitors—women passing through who needed to be quartered with us, the occasional addition or subtraction of a student, a religious scholar or two ushered in by Hejjiye for a lecture on some Friday. That was all. Do I make you feel that I resented or regretted the diminishment of my life, the festivals with all colour shot out of them, the world that had become much more constrained and constraining, the restrictive routines in the orphanage? If I do, I am imposing on my account those nebulous feelings that were yet to take shape in me. At that moment, I am afraid, I did not feel impoverished; I felt relieved.

You look startled. It is impossible for you to contemplate the life I led in the orphanage as something that could be welcome to me, or to anyone from your wider world. I understand you. And how I wish I could make you understand what I felt then. That is more difficult. How can it be possible to feel relief at the diminishment of your life? But it is. See, think of it in this way, think of that iPhone you have in front of you. Maybe you can understand the way I felt if you think back to a time when you—your generation knew such a time—did not have mobiles, did not have iPhones or the Internet. Can you remember a time like that? You can? Well, then, answer me: aren't there moments when you miss that old world of telephone lines? That world when, I am told, you had to find a telephone to make a call, you were not eternally connected to everyone, always at the entire world's beck and call. I have been told by older people that they miss that simpler world at times. You do too? Well, then maybe you can understand me: I was suddenly back in a simpler world I had only imagined. Perhaps it had never existed. How would I know? But it did exist there, at least for the first few weeks, in the orphanage: a world where things appeared to have meaning, because they were not refracted into a million distorted shapes in thousands of mirrors of perception, sensation, thought. No, I would be lying to you if I were to say that I regretted the impoverishment of my world, because it was at the same time a simplification and ordering of it—and, around that time, I even saw it as a kind of purification. I felt that the dross of existence was falling off me, leaving only what was essential.

HALIDE

Halide had been used to more festivals and definitely more colourful festivals than I was. That much was obvious to me from the first week I shared with her; she was moved into my room the day Ameena left. Halide complained to others about elements that she felt were lacking, reminiscing about how a particular festival or occasion would be celebrated in her Turkish town. I had grown up in a country where people neither shared nor cared about my festivals, but Halide had grown up among Muslims of her kind and she was used to discussing religious matters openly. She was also younger. She would get excited as a festival drew nearer and then be unable to hide her disappointment if it was not celebrated because it was not considered Islamic enough, or if it was celebrated differently from what she had been used to.

Almost the only festival that, I think, did not disappoint her entirely was Eid al-Adha. As the animal for the sacrifice had to be chosen in advance and, according to some preachers, brought up with care in the days before the event, this festival should have been preceded, as it had been in Halide's Turkish village, with a trip to the market. That year Hejjiye had calculated the various portions of sacrifice demanded and determined to buy a camel for the occasion. We all contributed the money from the little we had tucked away or were paid by Hejjiye, except for those girls who were destitute and those women whose menfolk elsewhere would perform the sacrifice on their behalf.

There was a buzz of excitement about a month before Eid, when Hejjiye asked the teachers and students if we wanted to go to the market with her. Of course almost everyone wished to. Evidently, it had been permitted in the previous years. Hejjiye had in mind a particular day when a cattle market was held. Villagers from the region would bring their poultry and cattle for sale in the town square, in preparation for Eid. The market started at dawn and lasted until sunset. Some girls, who had grown up in the town before becoming orphaned, had childhood memories of the market, and they spoke ceaselessly about it during mealtimes.

Hejjiye planned that we would reach the marketplace around ten. You would have enjoyed the scene, these droves of veiled women organised into bands, walking down the narrow road, across the barren fields and into the Town, some of the menfolk meeting or escorting their wives, daughters, and mothers. I am imagining it for you. That was the plan. It did not take place. We never went to the cattle market.

Hejjiye informed us the day before the outing that it would not be organised, after all. The girls had been very excited at the prospect. Some of them had not been out of the orphanage since being taken there. They did not hide their disappointment for once. But Halide was the only person who complained. "Why not?" she demanded, "Why can't we go out fully veiled and with you as our guardian?"

Hejjiye was nonplussed at the query and spoke about the distance, the danger, and so on. Remember the air raid in Khansa, a village in northeastern Syria, about a year ago, which killed a few dozen animals and about thirty people?

That was afterward but it had been a cattle market too. It got into the news because so many people died, but there had been similar incidents in markets—with casualties of four or five that almost never get reported internationally—and we had heard of them. Assad was never particular about where his bombs fell! I guess something like that could have happened to us. All of us always lived, by then, with that possibility, though it was to get worse over the next few months. But this was Eid, and it was as if we had all decided to pretend that the times were normal. The disappointment was difficult to hide. And, to be honest, at least some of us realised that the trip had been cancelled because Daesh had clamped down harder on women going out without male relatives, even if they were in a group. Even Hejjiye, married to the local commander, had to kowtow.

Hejjiye found a way round it. She asked her husband to organise a group of Bedouins to herd some cattle up to the orphanage. They came with some sheep, a couple of goats, and camels. The men of the Bedouin families stayed outside while the women—three of them, all in their fifties or older—came into our courtyard. The gate was opened for them to herd the animals in; it was the first time it had been opened since I had arrived. It had small wheels at the bottom, which were rusted and squealed. With the women and their animals inside, the gate was shut again and we were allowed to go out into the courtyard. Hejjiye went around from Bedouin to Bedouin bargaining for the two camels. It was obvious that she had trouble understanding the women. She had me with her—she liked keeping me with her—and she would occasionally comment on matters in English to me.

What she had most trouble with were the words that the sellers used for "camel." There appeared to be at least a dozen words, maybe more. The Bedouin women almost never called two camels by the same name. I had never thought of that: for me, there was just one word for the animal, "camel." In English. In Urdu, it was "oont," just one word again. Even in Arabic, I knew of only two words—one for the singular and one for the plural. But that was obviously not the case with the Bedouins. They didn't just have different names for different breeds, they even had specific names for different colours, for riding and herding camels, and, it appeared, for camels in different phases and years of their lives. It was like the Inuit having, as I recalled reading somewhere, about thirty names for "snow." What surprised me was that most of these different terms for camels—by age, sex, purpose, colour, breed—were unknown to Hejjiye too. Then I understood: like me and Ameena, she was basically a city person. She must have understood it too: she asked one of the older, local women to take over the bargaining.

We ended up purchasing two camels and a goat for Eid.

***

Eid was still about three weeks off. All of us believed—though, obviously, this is something that cannot be practised in cities—that the animals chosen for sacrifice have to be cared for and kept nearby. You cannot ask someone else to feed the animals, at least in the last few days, because, as you might recall, Abraham was commanded by God to sacrifice his most precious possession. A degree of care has to be invested in the animal to be sacrificed. I had heard and read this argument, but I had never taken it seriously. Neither, being a city person, had Hejjiye.

But Halide had. When Hejjiye instructed the Bedouin women to take the selected animals away and hand them over to the men outside, who would take care of them and the sacrifice, Halide objected.

"But they have to be kept here. We have to take care of our own animals," she said.

Hejjiye knew Halide was right in a narrowly Islamic way, and finally it was settled that the camels would be cared for elsewhere, while the goat would remain in the courtyard. This provided us with a pet, but it was mostly Halide who took care of the goat. It was an unusually frisky animal, often willing to lower its horns and do mock charges at people in its vicinity. Halide gave it a name: "Kaplan." What does it mean, I asked her. "Oh, it means tiger in Turkish," she laughed, "Don't you think it is a ferocious little thing?"

Halide would also, when she could, go out and whisper in Turkish to the goat. When I asked her about it, she said, in her sombre manner, "But of course animals understand what you say. They just do not speak. Every good farmer knows that."

**

In the beginning, when we still had Internet access, Halide and I often sneaked into the Internet room and surfed for news and sometimes even entertainment late in the nights. This was not really forbidden: we had four computers in the room, including my laptop, which I had left there, and they were used during the daytime to access preaching and Daesh postings, and sometimes to follow the news, though

the latter was always rigorously monitored by the chaperones. We were shown news that would be of use to us, and
nothing that was considered "degenerate" or "Western." For
instance, when the Chapel Hill shooting took place (this
was, actually, only a few months before we lost the Internet
for good), we were taken to watch it being reported or discussed a number of times. Always, Hejjiye would be there,
and would point out how the killings of the three Muslim
college students illustrated the Islamophobia of the West,
and also its hypocrisy—for Americans did not even see the
shootings as an act of Islamophobia, let alone that of terror
against American Muslims. But I am anticipating matters;
this was much later—Ameena was back with us when the
Chapel Hill killings took place. And Halide was … She was,
well, I guess I should come to it gradually. It is hard for me
to talk of what happened to Halide.

But in those months, Halide filled the space left in my
life by Ameena's marriage. After the initial weeks, the text
messages and e-mails from Ameena gradually diminished,
too. This did not worry me too much: she had moved closer
to the frontline, and she had to be more careful about using
electronic media. Moreover, my relationship with Halide
was in some ways the reverse of the relationship I had with
Ameena. Even though I still prided myself on returning
Ameena to her faith, rescuing her from the well-meaning
but surely misdirected influence of her parents, she had,
years ago, taken the upper hand in matters of faith. Despite
her limited Arabic, or maybe because of it, she had read
voraciously. Being the type of person who had to take a clear
stand on issues, she had moved on to a form of Islam—nar-
rowed down and honed to a few essential elements she had

imbibed from books and preachings of a certain sort—that actually had less space for even the few lived impurities that permeated the austere faith of my parents. Her Islam, when I look back on it today, was an ideological matter, while my parents had just been orthodox or conservative.

Halide was different. She was about a year younger than me. A thin girl, with thick glasses that made her look plainer than she was, and curly reddish-brown hair, she had been brought up with strong faith in Islam as a religion of justice and brotherhood. She had practised the faith all her life, in ways that reminded me of my own upbringing but with one central difference—she had grown up in Turkey and had not felt like an oddity or monster because of her faith. Like me, though, and unlike Ameena, she was willing to allow herself more leeway in some matters. Ameena had stopped watching any TV show or listening to music—even religious music was banned around us—and she did not give a second thought to such matters. Halide, like me, did not really see the harm of the occasional entertainment or frivolity, as long as it was not vulgar. That is, what we considered vulgar.

I think I should explain this further; I doubt that you are the kind of person who would understand someone like Halide. You might think—as so many in the West do—that we were just pining for inane MTV programmes and Hollywood films, that we were repressed by others or repressing ourselves. No, we were not. We did not find the sight of hips and bosoms heaving and thrusting along the same chant of sex-as-love in a hundred pop songs very new or interesting. We found situations in Hollywood films—for instance, where the hero or the heroine is surrounded by villains and fights his or her way out with computerised elegance—so predictable that we wondered how intelligent people could watch this same situation, repeated a thousand times in a hundred films, often in slow motion, and still consider it interesting or suspenseful? Halide and I had grown up with these films and songs around us, and we had long ago lost any interest in them, if we had ever found them interesting, which is doubtful, at least in my case.

So, what I have in mind is different. For me, music had merely been in the backdrop, playing somewhere, in class or at a function, for we had seldom listened to even religious *qawwalis* in my family. But Halide sorely missed Amitabh Bachchan's action dramas—where the Indian superhero righted the wrongs of the world—that her parents or older siblings had watched occasionally, as well as her favourite *anasheed* singers. I also think that, around the time, I had started missing the wider expanse of news—news that I had, when in England, dismissed as prejudiced and propagandist. I still did not trust the Western media—I doubt I would trust it fully even today—but I could not help noticing that the spectrum of opinions it covered was far wider and more varied than anything we were allowed to access during the daytime in our jihadi orphanage.

But, when we snuck back into the Internet room on the nights when we had electricity, we did not dare check such options: if we were caught, the consequences would have been drastic. There was nothing wrong in using the room at night, though no one else seemed to do so, but obviously it would be far more difficult if we were caught watching something Hejjiye had clearly dubbed un-Islamic or simply wrong. Moreover, there were no earphones available in the room—I guess on purpose—and we could not play the sound out aloud. Instead, we would sometimes surf for news and watch old silent films. Halide discovered Charlie Chaplin around that time, and fell in love with his films on YouTube. Sometimes she had to stuff her scarf into her mouth in order to prevent herself from screaming with laughter.

***

You will recall that 2014 had been a year of euphoria for the jihadis, until the coalition bombings started. By 2015, things were not the same, though Daesh was still firmly entrenched in the region around the orphanage and we kept on being told stories of victory and sacrifice. I didn't know if it was true or not, but Hejjiye regularly spoke of the dozens, hundreds, thousands of Muslims waiting to join us, not to mention the thousands of non-Muslims who were about to convert to the true faith. Did she believe in it? Did I believe in her? I think such questions cease to matter when you are situated as we were; to cease to believe in your mind would have been to cease to exist in your own heart. I wanted to exist.

Looking back, I can see that there was evidence of things changing from at least early in 2015: for instance, our rations were cut. Luxury items like Nutella became difficult to obtain. The quality of the food we prepared for distribution in town deteriorated (rice full of stones that took hours to sieve, coarser flour, and so on), and then its quantity diminished. There was less tailoring to do; less wool to knit. And yet I persevered in my heart. I never believed in all that Hejjiye said—I knew that even the best of human beings get carried away by their own hopes and dreams—but I trusted in the broad outlines, and I believed that I was helping Hejjiye and the jihadis fight the good fight, as the Americans might put it.

And I was; many of them, like me, were fighting the good fight. But you know when a good fight becomes evil? I realised this much later. (You can write this down.) I don't think all your brilliant, pontificating philosophers, who think of goodness and evil as concepts but have never stared either in the face, I don't think any of your philosophers and editors can come up with a better definition of evil: evil, I am certain now, arises whenever a person believes that only what he considers purely good has the right to exist. I have thought about it: why did Allah have to create Shaitan, God have to create Satan? Why create evil? We were told then—as I was told at home—that it was to test humanity. But why test humanity if you are all-powerful and purely good? Why not just drench humanity in pure goodness, as if in your divine rays? The answer—don't laugh at me—that I have now is this: evil is a precondition to goodness. Goodness reveals itself only in its capacity to tolerate the pettiness and dullness of evil. Goodness has to live with the possibility of evil, not eradicate it. As long as it does so, the evil that confronts goodness stays petty, dull, limited, essentially unimportant. But when goodness wants to become pure and alone, that is when it turns evil, truly evil; not the grubby evil that it has to tolerate in order to be goodness, but Evil itself.

This is something I have thought of only in recent months. In those days, as I told you, I still believed in the good fight. But soon my belief in our good fight was to be shaken. It had to do with Halide.

***

I have told you that Halide and I, and some others like us, were basically teachers in that orphanage, supervised by

Hejjiye, who was foster mother, spiritual advisor, and principal. Students had been passing through our classes. Once in a while a girl would disappear and we would be told that she had married a jihadi. In one case, a wedding took place in the orphanage too, not very different from the one that had been organised for Ameena. But, mostly, two or three girls would leave every month, and we would be informed that they had been happily married. More girls would come and, as the war drew closer again, widows and wives and mothers of jihadis. In some ways, we were a kind of caravanserai for the relocating the womenfolk of dead or injured jihadis.

Sometimes one of the orphans who had left would be celebrated as having "martyred" herself for the cause. The assumption was that the girl had blown herself up as a suicide bomber on one of the frontlines. We would say special prayers for her soul. Hejjiye might give an extra talk that day. And then things would proceed as they had: the classes, the prayers, the talks, the discussions, the chores, the meals.

It all started to change for me one night when Halide was browsing through Turkish news sites, as she often did. We never really read the pages, simply glancing at the headlines and moving on, immediately deleting the site from the "history" column if it was a controversial publication. Suddenly, Halide gasped, and indicated to me to keep watch from the door. By this I knew that she was surfing a forbidden site, not just an unusual one. I did so. Then, despite my growing irritation and nervousness as I stood by the door, Halide read various news items for the next twenty minutes or so. I kept waving to her to stop. Whatever it was, I knew it could get us in trouble. But Halide, usually obedient to a fault, ignored me. When she conceded to my frantic, silent urging and finally left the computer, I did not want to stay any longer in the room, and we went back to our bedroom.

Halide looked shaken, but she did not say anything to me.

***

The next day Halide told Hejjiye that she was ill and could not teach her class. It might seem to you that isolated as we were, we probably had lots of time to spare. But, as I have said, we didn't. Our day was packed. From the moment we got up at dawn to say the first prayer, all of us followed a similar routine: prayers, Quran reading sessions, talks by Hejjiye, occasional guest lectures, cleaning, cooking, preparing whatever we were asked to prepare for the men fighting the jihad (food packets, bandage rolls, etc.), classes, workshops, other chores, communal meals from the same large plates. We were divided into teams of women and students. Daily chores were circulated on a weekly basis between the teams. All this was worked out by Hejjiye, who had a chart hanging in her office, and I still do not know to what extent the routines were common to other places and to what extent they were Hejjiye's doing. I now feel that our orphanage was partly Hejjiye's creation, and probably not typical of Daesh organisation. In any case, from dawn to dusk, we seldom had more than half an hour to rest. We always had our last meal after dusk, and then we were free to be on our own, but mostly expected to keep each other company. Caroms was the only game that we were allowed to play; cards had been banned a long time back, I was told. Some of the girls played a game in which a ring would be passed around behind the backs of the members of a team, while a member of the opposing team had to deduce who was holding the ring through what appeared to me to be a relentless flow of inane patter. But, in general, we frowned upon such frivolities.

***

Halide returned to her chores and classes, but I could see that she spent less and less time with us, preferring to go out and whisper to the goat, which was getting tame and fat in preparation for the sacrifice. It had taken to clambering up the trunk of the olive tree, so Halide spoke to it almost eye to eye. But she hardly spoke to us. She was particularly sullen with Hejjiye and her chaperones, and I noticed that she often made careful comments about Islam that wrong-footed them.

Have I described Halide to you? I haven't; no, not really. Yes, I have said that she was a bit younger than me, but actually she looked a lot younger: she had the almost flat figure of a girl of twelve or thirteen, and the rimmed glasses that she wore made her look both younger and more serious at the same time. Like a small girl pretending to be a woman. She had told me enough about herself for me to put together a jigsaw of her past: younger daughter in a family of farmers, her parents die (she did not say how, but it was obviously sudden), she is handed around from married sibling to sibling, until she becomes the responsibility of the older sister, married to a jihadi, who brings her here and leaves her. Halide had told me that she wanted to be part of the orphanage; like me and Ameena, she wanted to help in the good fight. So, it was not as if she had been abandoned here by her siblings, though one part of me wondered, even then, if they had not manipulated her into this decision partly to get rid of her. Halide struck me as a person easy to control and shape. She was to surprise me in just a few weeks.

***

Despite the fact that Halide had taken care of the goat, it was some of the girls and I who had to restrain ourselves when, on the morning of Eid, the goat was taken away, bleating, as if it could sense its death, to be sacrificed. When the meat from the sacrifices was brought to us to be cooked—after portions had been distributed to the poor—I found it difficult to even pretend to eat. Halide, on the other hand, ate normally.

Lying in bed, I quizzed her later that evening. I asked her indirectly, of course; we were all careful with each other about matters of faith. I said to her, "Halide, don't you miss the goat?"

"Little Kaplan?" she replied. "Of course I miss little Kaplan."

"You did not seem to," I replied. "You had a better appetite than me tonight."

"But," she looked surprised, "that is something else. You have to care for the animal you sacrifice; you have to love it. Why should you offer Allah a sacrifice that means nothing to you?"

But the answer seemed to make her thoughtful, and she turned her back to me and lay there in her bed, staring at the wall. She would do so when she did not want to talk.

***

The controversy burst upon us a few days later. I was called into Hejjiye's office. It was a large room, once a classroom, whose walls still had signs of framed photos or paintings that had been removed and burnt after the Daesh took over these parts. There was an executive table, with built-in drawers, and leather chairs at the end of the room, on the wall behind which hung a huge black Daesh flag. This was the only place in the building that bore any Daesh insignia; even the men in the guardhouse outside dressed like locals and did not put out flags or banners. I realised that our orphanage contained too many daughters and wives of jihadis—widows, orphans, or even married women with no immediate family—and the Daesh did not want to draw attention to it.

Hejjiye's office was much larger, but not different in a generic manner from the principal's office to which Mrs. Chatterji had sent me just … no, I no longer wanted to count the days—each a century—from that event to this place. There was a file cabinet on one side and a three-seat leather sofa and a coffee table on the other.

Hejjiye gestured to me to sit in the sofa. Then she joined me with two cups of coffee, poured from a thermos on her desk. She did not beat about the bush.

"It is about Halide," she said, "Has she been talking to you?"

I knew it was something serious; Halide had been bearing around some burden for weeks now. But she had not said much to me, unless I were to talk of her slight impatience, at times, with Hejjiye and her crowd, expressed more in a grimace than with a word. It seemed unnecessary to mention her impatience to Hejjiye. I pretended to misunderstand her.

"Yes," I replied, "We lie in bed at times and she talks about her family."

"And …?" Hejjiye encouraged me.

"She appears to have been very close to her parents, especially her father. She was only nine when they died. Very devout people, they were, it appears to me. She venerates their memory."

"That's all? Hasn't she discussed anything about recent events?"

"The news sometimes, the plight of Muslims in the world. You know, the sort of things we talk about over meals."

"Nothing else?"

"What else could she have spoken about?"

Hejjiye gave me a penetrating look. Then she said, "No, I guess she won't talk about such matters to you. She knows you will not agree."

"What matters?"

"She has been saying things to the girls, in her classes. Things that are surprising, coming from one of us."

"Like?"

"You know, Jamilla," Hejjiye said suddenly, laying a hand over mine, "You know that women have a role to play in our struggle."

I nodded.

"Our role is as wives, mothers, daughters. You know, I keep urging you to marry, for example, marry like your friend, Ameena, did. Marry a jihadi."

"I will, Hejjiye," I reassured her, as I always did when the subject cropped up. "One day."

"That is what you say every time!" she laughed. "You know our jihadis need wives. Anyway, we will talk about that some other time. It is Halide we need to discuss."

"Is it something about her getting married?"

"Married?" Hejjiye was surprised. "No, not that I know of."

"I don't know what else she could have spoken of to the girls."

"No, you don't. You are not the gossipy, frivolous kind, or you would have heard. Well, it is about a believing woman's duty. You know that some of our girls, the ones who do not marry, and sometimes girls who marry and lose their husbands, you know that they sometimes offer themselves to the cause."

I made the standard response: "May Allah grant them paradise!"

"Surely they will be rewarded. It might not be what women were made for, but these are difficult times, and such women are to be praised."

"Alhamdhulillah!" I agreed.

"Halide does not think so," Hejjiye said, abruptly. She observed me.

My surprise must have shown. I had never realised that Halide would be so bold as to make a statement like that. Hejjiye was satisfied with my response.

"Yes, I was shocked too. Three different girls reported it to me. They said, Halide told them not to kill themselves for any reason, because suicide is repugnant to Allah."

I did not know what to say. Deep down, I agreed with Halide. I was not alone in the conviction. But I also believed, in those days, that the girls who killed themselves only attacked our sworn enemies and I reasoned, uncertain but still groping to retain my faith, that they did not take innocent lives. I shook my head in silence.

"Speak to her, Jamilla. Speak to Halide. Get her to stop. Or I will have to tell others. I cannot ignore another report."

I could not refuse Hejjiye's request. But I did not want to speak to Halide; I was afraid of what I might find out. Many of us had come to live with this inhibition from knowing the other too well; it was too much of a responsibility and we had enough to cope with in our own hearts and minds. But, of course, I could not refuse Hejjiye's request. It was not a request; I knew it was a command.

***

I asked Halide that very night, as we lay in bed. That was the only time we were alone together in any case, late at night, as we tried to sleep. I remember that it was one of the last quiet nights in the Town; the war was still some distance from us. That was going to change. Soon the nights were to be punctuated with the sound of gunfire and bomb blasts, the drone of planes, which drew nearer and nearer each week, until … But I will get to that. The night I am talking about was still. As the orphanage was some distance from the Town and the houses across the football field on the other side were abandoned ruins, I guess it was even quieter in our rooms. There were frequent electricity outages now, and the backup generator was used only for emergencies. Our evenings had sunk into the ancient rhythm of the countryside: we retired after dark, huddling in our rooms, saying our prayers, but basically preparing for sleep. That there were towns, cities elsewhere where lights would be burning and people out on the streets until after midnight seemed unimaginable, even to me.

We had just said the last prayer and were lying in bed. It was then that I asked Halide. I had been worrying about how to ask her but, at the last moment, I just blurted out about my conversation with Hejjiye.

Halide lay there staring at the ceiling for at least two minutes after I had finished speaking. Just when I thought that she had decided not to answer me, she said, "It is wrong."

I turned around and propped myself up on my elbows. "What is wrong?" I asked her.

She started speaking, and the words fell in a torrent from her. She switched from English to Arabic, sometimes even said a few things in Turkish. Often I lost her, and had to ask her to repeat herself or slow down. But the gist of it became clear to me. Halide had decided that the girls in the orphanage were either being groomed to marry jihadis—she had no objection to that—or to carry out suicide attacks. I knew this much too, but I had seen the matter as a personal choice. Halide, on the other hand, argued that this was an institution in which there were just three kinds of women: older women, who were teachers or related to jihadis who were not around to protect them or had recently died; younger women who were meant to be brides; and women, mostly girls, who were being trained to be suicide bombers. I protested that she was seeing too much system in it. She laughed and said, "Believe what you may, but why do you think some girls are taught specifically by Hejjiye and her women? They are being indoctrinated to carry out suicide attacks."

I refused to believe her. It sounded too much like the sort of conspiracy that the far right in Europe kept dreaming up. I still think she was at least partly wrong; that such things happened was not the result of a plan but the consequence of circumstances. But, in any case, that was not Halide's problem; her problem was the suicide bombers.

"It is wrong to commit suicide. You know that," she said to me.

I knew that. I told her that we all knew that, even Hejjiye. But we knew that these suicide bombers were used only as a last resort, and only against our sworn enemies. Surely, Allah would forgive them for killing themselves to save all believers, I said, as I had been conditioned to think and say.

"Maybe," said Halide, "Maybe. But will Allah forgive them for killing innocent people?"

"You know that they do not set out to kill innocent people," I replied. This was also a conditioned reply. You may wonder at my stupidity in believing this lie for so long, but all of us did—and in many ways we were not that different from people like you who might want to believe that the hundreds of civilians killed by Western government forces are just "mistakes," simply "collateral damage." I argued this out with Halide.

She was not willing to be convinced. She told me that her eyes had been opened by a report—the night when she had surfed while I kept a worried lookout in the Internet room. It had featured photos of some victims of a recent attack in Syria or Turkey (I never dared check which one), and Halide had recognised the faces of two girls—twins—she had gone to school with, when staying with one of her siblings. "I knew those girls. They were good girls, religious girls," she added.

I tried to convince her that mistakes happen; we were fighting a war.

Halide was quietly obdurate. No, she said, she had checked, there were too many "mistakes," and in any case, she was convinced that it was wrong to teach the girls to kill themselves. She would tell them so; she had been telling them so. She would not have their deaths on her head; Allah would hold her accountable. She could not ignore what might be happening here, even if—as I claimed—she did not have concrete proof. She would tell the girls at every possible opportunity what she thought was right.

I was horrified. I urged her not to do so. But Halide refused to listen.

"You know that this could end badly, Halide. Very badly," I burst out in desperation. How did I know it could? I had been lying to myself all along that we were the good ones, that we only did what was good. Had one part of me known that any such claim is itself a way to justify oppression, that it is required only when, deep down, we know that we are complicit in wrongdoing?

"Don't say anything to the girls you do not know well, Halide," I begged her, "I don't want anything to happen to you. What will I do without you?"

Halide got up and took my face between her palms. I think there must have been tears in my eyes. She kissed me on my forehead, as if she was many decades older than me.

"Don't worry about me," she said, "My parents will be there for me. They are always with me."

***

No. I did not report the conversation to Hejjiye. She asked me at least three times over the next week or so. I take some pride in the fact that I lied to her. I told her that Halide had not said anything unusual to me.

But that was not enough to save Halide. Other girls complained; this was a set-up where the structure of authority encouraged you to run down the weak and the vulnerable and to cater to the powerful. And who was even half as powerful in the orphanage as Hejjiye?

The next two weeks run like a horror film in my head. I see the main scenes recurring again and again, and sometimes I still wake up, sweating, desperate and unable to do anything to help Halide.

First, there was the public humiliation of Halide. We had an assembly. Halide was called up and asked by Hejjiye, if it was true that she had told girls X, Y, and Z—they were named and identified—that it was wrong to kill yourself for Allah. Halide did not say anything in reply. Then the girls came up one after another and repeated what Halide had reportedly said to them. Halide was asked again, and this time she replied, in a clear calm voice, as if she had made up her mind: "I was taught to believe that Muslims neither kill themselves nor kill those who are innocent. I was taught that the Prophet, peace be upon him, said that to kill one innocent person is the equivalent of destroying the world."

Hejjiye and her chaperones took over from there. They browbeat Halide; the accused her; they heckled her; they made her a laughable object in the eyes of many of the girls, as she increasingly grew nervous and incoherent in her answers. Finally, after about an hour of this, they ordered her to be secluded from the rest of us. It was then that I discovered why there was this room, with a barred gate instead of a wooden door, at the end of our wing. I have told you that it was the only room with its own toilet. It was a cell. It must have been used for a similar purpose in the past; now, Halide was put in it.

Every morning she would be taken out by Hejjiye or her chaperones, brought into our breakfast assembly, and asked to recant and repent. She would refuse. She would then be abused; some girls even started pelting her with rubbish. The first week, one meal a day was given to her; then even that was discontinued. I managed to smuggle bread to her twice, but it was difficult. After four days without food, she could not walk on her own and had to be helped to the assembly. Finally, even that stopped, and Halide lay in the cell.

At the end of these days, after Halide had been lying alone in her cell for at least two days, Hejjiye suddenly announced that she had received permission from Halide's sister to arrange the girl's marriage to a jihadi. God was to be praised! We were told to provide meals to Halide. The next day she was taken out of her cell. She could still not walk on her own. She was helped to the gate by Hejjiye and some other women from town, one of whom was supposed to be Halide's relative. Halide looked dazed. She did not even look at me as she passed us. She had not chosen to leave or marry—would it even be a marriage, I wondered, and was suddenly frightened that my doubt could be overheard—and, hence, she chose not to look at us, at me. Yes, at me. I felt that in my very bones. I knew it.

The door in the gate opened with a metallic clank and the women passed through it, supporting Halide. That is the last time I saw Halide. No one ever mentioned her in the orphanage, and I never had the courage to ask Hejjiye. Moreover, that very evening the war returned to the town.

We had heard planes in the past. Recently we had even heard some gunshots and blasts that did not sound too far off. But the town had not been bombed, at least since I had arrived.

That evening, just as we were doing our ablutions for the sunset prayer, we heard the sound of planes. We rushed out to the veranda, and peered out from between the grilles. There were three planes. They were flying low, and the last vestiges of sunlight glinted off them. They passed us heading for the town, and soon there was the sound of bombs falling and anti-aircraft fire. Dark smoke plumes rose over the town roofs. The planes flew on, and disappeared.

THE PRISONERS

The character of Hejjiye's orphanage changed with the war returning to our parts. First, Hejjiye and some of her women who lived in town moved in with us. There was more than enough space in the sprawling orphanage building to accommodate them. Then, slowly, other women started trickling in, some of them tired and dejected, some full of vehemence at the government forces, at the Shia militia, at America. As the sound of the fighting drew closer day by day, and planes or helicopters were heard more often, it looked like we were a place of refuge; the reputation of the orphanage was expected to keep us from getting bombed.

Some women had brought their livestock into the courtyard with them, and slowly the place started resembling a village more than a school. There were chickens running about and, once, even a couple of sheep. However, the animals and birds did not last: they were sold by their owners for money, and in any case, there was very little to feed them. Grain was getting scarcer. The water supply would often be interrupted, and there were days when we had to pull up the slightly brackish water of the well in the courtyard. The shrubs around the well had already been grazed bare by Halide's Kaplan; the gnarled olive tree had lost much of its foliage and all the sparrows that once nestled in it. Only the pigeons continued to flutter down and flap away, as they always had.

***

I tried not to think of Halide. There had also been little news of Ameena; the last time she had posted on her jihadi Facebook page was a few weeks ago. Remember, Internet service was quite irregular by then. I was now feeling lonely in that place. I was afraid to confront even my own doubts, and of course there was no one I could share them with. The fact that Hejjiye lived with us also meant that I was often called to her; this enhanced my prestige in the eyes of the others, but her company was a strain to me now: I had to maintain a steady level of enthusiasm about the cause—Hejjiye's enthusiasm never wavered, not even when she got worried about her husband in town because he had not contacted her for four days or when one of her brood (I could never distinguish between her children and her co-wives) took ill. There was something admirable about it. Or there was something robotic about it. Sometimes, Hejjiye reminded me of those models on a catwalk—an expression pasted on their faces, perfect posture, incredible balance, eyes revealing nothing. You watch them promenade and wonder if they can still distinguish between their show and reality—if there ever was a difference in their minds? Nothing could be more dissimilar outwardly—Hejjiye, who always dressed with propriety, and these models, who wear the vestiges of men's fancies—and yet I feel convinced now that, inwardly, they resembled each other. The orphanage— or maybe the Islamic State itself—was Hejjiye's catwalk.

But it was difficult, even for Hejjiye, to maintain a façade of normality as the bombs started coming closer, and sometimes there were alarms, when the men in the guardhouses would take cover. The place was also getting crowded, and at first I thought that Hejjiye organised a mass wedding just to get rid of some of the girls. I now realise that it could not have been the main reason: the jihadis were getting desperate for wives in 2015. I am sure Hejjiye did not have a choice.

I have told you that Hejjiye liked marrying off her girls to jihadis. But, with the exception of what had happened to Halide, this was always done with the clear consent of the girls. This time, fifteen girls were told to get prepared—at least some of them were not expecting the command—to be married. Consent had been obtained from their guardians, Hejjiye announced. That seemed to settle it. We did not know their guardians; we did not inquire.

Some of the girls were sent off to town—or other places—for their weddings. But four girls—having no family in the vicinity—were married off at the orphanage, with the jihadis sitting outside, in the guardhouse, and the imam entering by the gate to get the women's consent. If weddings in the past had been meagre, this one was totally shorn of any joy. Some dates were distributed, and then the jihadis drove off with their new wives, veiled and, in at least one case, wailing. But even the wailing was meagre, for she could not allow herself to show too much grief either.

Meagreness. As I look at the décor of this restaurant, where I sit talking to you, and at the lushness of the trees outside, I think back to my days in England—yes, even to the grubby, grey building of my ordinary school, netted from the streets with high wire, as I told you—and it all seems teeming, colourful, and rich to me now compared to what I saw in Syria. What I saw were cold white walls. Perhaps you can sense it in my account of the place. Hejjiye's orphanage was both sanctuary and prison for us. There had been those vivid medieval tiles on the walls outside, but inside, it was spare and white, with wooden panels of colonial wiring. A well and bush in the meagre courtyard, some straggly birds. The sandy soil. Cracks in the floors. Shuttered windows, barred verandas. Not one picture on the walls, nothing but the black flag in Hejjiye's office. True, what I had seen of Syria had been limited to our journey—but even then, where were the glorious mosques, the teeming streets and souks that I had read about in my books in England? I was nowhere. Simplicity, I called it then; meagreness is the word I think of now. Our circumstances and lives were meagre, and my description of them must sound spare to you. Time seemed to slow down, but only for a while.

***

Then someone pressed the forward button on our lives. Women and children came and left more frequently; the town and adjoining villages were bombed regularly. Hejjiye's rules still served as the glue that held together our secluded community, but they were fraying with the new arrivals. In particular, I recall an evening when a middle-aged woman who had arrived in a group sat on a bed, rocking slightly, repeating the same phrase—"O my son, my son!" Despite the injunctions of Hejjiye that excessive mourning was not Islamic and her assurance that Allah was great, the woman's keening poured out into the comfortless night until, around dawn, she finally fell asleep from exhaustion.

Then the rumours got worse, and we heard that Peshmerga forces had breached Daesh defences in a neighbouring town. They had even captured some villages in the region.

One night we were woken up by loud banging on the gate. The moon was out. It was the desert moon, larger than it appears elsewhere, brighter than the sun had been on some days in England. It shed a strange light on everything, erasing the signs of ugliness, as if absolving the buildings and fields of human folly. You have to experience the moon in those parts. No, it is not just the Muslim in me speaking.

I and a couple of other women hastily put on our veils and ran into the courtyard with Hejjiye. This had never happened before. We were all frightened. But Hejjiye was used to assuming command. She shouted to the guards outside, who reassured her that all was OK; it was just a convoy of Daesh.

"Why are you banging like madmen on our gate?" shouted Hejjiye across the metal gate. She must have been really shaken to use such words; we spoke to and of men with careful respect. In the silver moonlight, I could see Hejjiye's handsome face creased with worry.

"They have two women with them."

"Women? What women?"

"Peshmerga prisoners."

"Women prisoners?"

"Yes, the godless Kurds hide behind their women!"

"What is the world coming to?!"

"Your husband has commanded that these women be put in the cell that you have."

"Allah forbid! Let me talk to my husband."

"He is not here."

"Wait then; I will call him."

Hejjiye headed back to her office—she was using it as a bedroom now, sleeping on the sofa, with a couple of her women on mattresses in the room, while her co-wives and children had other rooms in the place. She must have managed to get her husband on her mobile; by then, we had been forbidden to use mobiles unless it was an emergency. She came out, not looking very happy about the situation, and ordered one of the women to put a couple of sheets in the cell. To me, she muttered in English, the only time she ever said anything even remotely critical of a Daesh decision: "One night we will all have our throats cut in our sleep by these women who want to be men!"

We were fully veiled by then, of course, as there was a chance that men might enter the courtyard. Hejjiye—who always kept all the keys in her fashionable Gucci handbag—had brought along the keys to the door in the gate. There were two locks on it. She unlocked both, pushed open the door, and stepped aside. It creaked, sounding eerily loud in the moonlit night.

Two women were pushed in. At first, we thought they were men. They were dressed like men. Then, as we noticed the chains on them, we realised that these were the soldiers. One of them was probably forty, broad without being fat, and she entered first. The other soldier looked like a young girl. Two Daesh soldiers came in with them. But they stopped there. It was Hejjiye and her women who took hold of the chains of the two women and led them—with a few curses, though Hejjiye forbade her women from spitting at the captives—to the cell. This was, you would remember, the cell where Halide had suffered for two weeks. To me, it was already an accursed space.

The two Peshmerga soldiers did not say anything when they were pushed in and the cell locked on them. Outside, on being signalled that all was well, the Daesh soldiers left the courtyard and we went back to our beds.

For a moment it felt like we had simply had more visitors.

It was only the next morning that reality sank in. The war was here: not just in town or around it, but in our orphanage with the blue-tiled walls, the huge metal gate, the courtyard, and the long dark wings of rooms and dormitories! We had two prisoners in our cell. The girls all wanted to go and see them, and Hejjiye had to put one of her women outside the cell to warn the girls away.

Why, you ask? Why were the women put in with us?

Well, at the moment, I thought that it was because this was the first time they had captured women soldiers in the region, and they simply did not know what to do. They needed time to find out. But later I wondered whether it was not more than that, whether they were not a kind of insurance against getting bombed, for instance. I must have told you that I had never met Hejjiye's husband; he was the commander of the town, and if he ever entered the orphanage, I was not told of it. Even now, there were only women inside the building (and some small boys); wives who wanted to spend time with their husbands, which was not often, took the risk of going to the town. Hejjiye had gone back once or twice after moving in with us. But her husband had never come inside. Still, not having met him, I had heard of him, and I had the impression that, like Hejjiye, he was an efficient and calculating person. I wonder whether he had not reasoned that the women prisoners would not just save us from brutal attacks; in case the enemy got closer, they could even be used to strike a bargain. And, actually, he was not wrong, as events were to show.

***

I was never the kind of person who provokes a confrontation. I realised all along that I was my mother's daughter and now I even did what she would had done: faced with an obstacle or something I did not agree with, I retreated into the Quran, which I read over and over again, and to domestic responsibilities. I would clean up, almost obsessively, go to the kitchen to help out even when it was not my turn, offer an extra lesson to someone, ask for permission to hear a preacher on DVD or computer (if he had Internet), and, inevitably, all the unexpected chores would be delegated to me: one of them was to take meals to the two Kurdish prisoners, and to wait until they had eaten, so that the plates and glasses were removed from them immediately. Hejjiye did not trust Kurds. But she also did not trust most of the women around her; on two occasions small groups of women had tried to pelt the Kurdish prisoners with filth and pebbles. To prevent this, she entrusted the meals for the women only to me, and posted two or three of her reliable lieutenants, including me, outside their cells. A bed was dragged up into the corridor for us to use. We even took turns sleeping there.

Initially, the Kurdish women had been hostile to me; the older woman spat in my direction a couple of times. I would simply ask them how they were in Arabic, and then sit there, outside the bars of the cell, and read some edifying tract or pamphlet. The older woman would often say something that seemed aimed at me, but as it was in Kurdish I did not understand it. I am sure she did not say polite things to me. Not that I minded; I had not lost my faith—I still have not—but I had lost my belief in the exact ways I had been brought up to follow my faith. It did not make sense anymore—this intense hatred and violence being practised in the name of a religion that stood for peace in its very name, this endless, nitpicking, bureaucratic intolerance being practised in the name of a God whose most common attributes, as I had been told from the time I was an infant, were mercy and forgiveness! As for these two Kurdish women, what could I say? I felt ashamed to sit in front of them, and if the older one had not abused me, as she obviously did, I would have found it intolerable.

The two women made me feel nostalgic about my school days for the first time: not just missing my family, which I had and still do, but missing all of it. They made me feel guilty toward the goodness I had not seen because pettiness had blinded me to it. How had I failed to register the many people who did accept me as I was, veiled and alien in their world, just because there were some who stared, or muttered, or shouted like that crazy woman in the bus? How had I failed to see the decency of parks with children, care for the weak and unemployed—for what can one call it but decency? How, I sometimes wondered with shock and pain, how had I failed to register this basic decency, simply because there were also idiots who excluded me and mine? Sometimes I lay awake late into the night, thinking of such matters—and now I no longer dared e-mail my true thoughts even to Ameena, let alone any of my other jihadi "friends." Is this what I had come to—the inability to trust even my best friend? If human beings cannot have faith in other human beings, despite all their mutual failures, then can they ever have faith in the Almighty, I wondered?

Yes, I was glad that the older Kurdish woman abused me.

***

But then, one evening, as I sat outside the bars, waiting for the prisoners to finish eating and shove the utensils back to me, I could feel that the two women kept looking at me and talking. I knew they were discussing me. Then the younger girl—she could not have been older than Halide—moved closer to the bars and said to me, in English, "You are not Turkish. You are American. No?"

I was so taken aback by the question, and the language it was put in, that I could only stammer that, yes, I was not a Turk, but I was not American either; I was from England. The girl translated it back to the older woman and they talked, excitedly, in Kurdish for a moment. Then the girl said to me, smiling a bit—it was the first time either of them had smiled at me: "She wants to know how you could leave England and come to work for these people?"

What could I say? I answered, even though it sounded a weak answer to me now: "I came to work for Allah."

The girl translated it back to the older woman, who uttered a dismissive laugh, and spoke quickly in response. The girl shook her head and said, "She wants me to ask you if you really think that Allah wants all this? That Allah wants women to be treated like slaves and Muslims to kill good human beings, even other Muslims?"

Once again, I did not know what to say. "Who knows what Allah wants?" I answered.

"Exactly!" barked the older woman. Evidently she understood a bit of English too.

***

After that, the younger woman would talk to me a bit during the single meal they were given every day, often interpreting for the older woman, whose name was Dilnaz. The younger one was called Sera. I had known that they were soldiers of the Kurdish army. Three times they were interrogated by groups of older Daesh men—though always in the silent presence of Hejjiye and some of us. All the women had to be veiled for the interrogations, which lasted about an hour each time; the rest of us were shut away in the other wing. But while we too had our faces covered, the Kurdish prisoners—who had to be threatened and made to put on a veil in the first place—were required to keep their faces exposed, so that the bearded interrogators could read their expressions. The same facts would be repeated over and over again. The prisoners would be asked about their forces. They would be asked to repent. They would be berated. They would be promised death in this life and retribution in the next. The interrogators—at least on the two occasions I was there, in the group with Hejjiye—were particularly interested in ascertaining Dilnaz's rank.

Sometimes Sera, the younger woman, would break down and start sobbing. But I never saw Dilnaz falter. When angry, she would look at the interrogators boldly, despite an order on one occasion that she be lashed for such "lewdness." Three lashes, administered immediately in the cell by one of the interrogators, after Dilnaz had been tied to a bed by us: they could lash her, kill her, even rape her, as they threatened, but they would not touch her! She would give her name and regiment, as would Sera. Both claimed to be common soldiers, holding ranks equivalent to that of a private. Yes, there were thousands of women like them. Yes, they were Muslims. No, they did not think Allah would punish them. No, she was not afraid of what Daesh might do. Yes, that is what she would call them—Daesh—whether they liked it or not. Wasn't she afraid of the violence men can do to women? Yes, she was—where is the woman who isn't, but what sort of man who takes the name of God would even speak of such things? No, she was not an officer; she was just a soldier. Yes, she was prepared to be executed. Why didn't they get it done with? She would walk out with them this very moment. Yes, Sera would too. No, don't think she is weak because she is sobbing. She is a Kurdish girl; she is not weak. Never underestimate a Kurdish woman, as you will find out soon, if you haven't yet, O you men of Daesh.

It was during these interrogations that I grew convinced that Dilnaz was not just a soldier. She had the authority of someone used to giving commands; the conviction of someone who was not just a follower of orders. Also, the way Sera deferred to her, the way Dilnaz sustained Sera, all this could not just be attributed to Dilnaz being older. Then, as Dilnaz spoke to me over meals, translated by Sera, I realised that the older woman had a much longer history of involvement in the Kurdish struggle. Once she revealed that both her parents had been officeholders of *Partiya Karkerên Kurdistanê*—PKK, the Kurdistan Workers' Party—and she had grown up with the struggle for a Kurdish homeland.

She did not say anything more, though. She was still watchful with me.

Then something even more momentous—for me—occurred. Ameena returned.

***

It was early morning. I had just finished saying the dawn prayer. What was the day? It was in April, I remember that. Ameena had left in September, as you recall. I had heard less and less from her over the past six months, and there had been no news at all the past three or four weeks. Actually, the way I remember it, around the time the Kurdish women were interred with us, Ameena had stopped communicating entirely. But then, with the Internet often gone, so had most of the rest of the world, and Ameena's silence was not unusual in that context.

Then, that April day at dawn, Hejjiye herself came to my room. This was just after breakfast, when we had a few moments of our own if we were not on the morning cleanup team. I had been alone there, after Halide was isolated and then married off. This must have been due to Hejjiye, because all the other rooms were now occupied, and even some of the closed student dormitories had been opened up, as more Daesh women and children arrived from the various frontlines.

Hejjiye always followed basic Western norms with me. She knocked on the half-closed door before coming in.

"Salaam-alaikum. Can I join you?" she asked.

What could I say? I wished her peace as well and made space on my bed. But Hejjiye sat down on the other one, bare and a bit dusty now that Halide was no longer there. I had a book lying on it, a commentary on the Quran in Arabic. I read such books now basically to improve my Arabic. Hejjiye picked it up, looked at the cover, and nodded approvingly. It was a sanctioned commentary. If it had been dangerous to read secular literature in Daesh regions last year, now it was perhaps even more dangerous to read certain orthodox scholars of Islam—many had been blacklisted as they, or their institutions, distanced themselves from Daesh.

"You know, Jamilla," said Hejjiye, as I had half expected her to (it was a common topic for her to raise with me), "You really should get married now."

"Soon, soon," I said, "As soon as we start winning our way to Baghdad again or take Damascus." These were the two "Daesh" goals I had set as a precondition to marrying, vows I had taken, I claimed—and I secretly prayed that they would never be met.

"We are winning," she corrected me immediately. "We are winning. Don't trust the rumours. There are just some minor setbacks because of bombings by the accursed Americans. Otherwise each of our men is more than a match for ten Peshmerga soldiers and twenty government turncoats."

"In truth," I replied in chaste Arabic, "How else can it be when Allah fights with them?"

"True, true. Allah is Great," she responded.

I waited. I knew that she had not come into my room for this predictable catechism. She picked up the commentary and put it down again.

"But you see, Jamilla," she finally continued, "the rumourmongers are busy; we have to disregard what they say."

"That is what I do," I responded. "You know me."

"You are a devout woman, Jamilla. You are unwavering in your faith. You will make a wonderful wife and a glorious mother. Yes, I know you; you are not to be swayed." Then after another pause, she added, "But even good women are swayed by rumours at times. Even good women. Your friend Ameena, for instance, a good woman, no doubt, but, well …"

I could not hide the look of horror and fear on my face. I gripped Hejjiye's hand and blurted out, "What happened? Has something happened to Ameena?"

She loosened herself from my grip and patted me on my head.

"No, no, nothing. Don't worry. She is fine. Nothing much. Ameena is on her way here. You will see her soon. It is just that she had a misunderstanding with Hassan; it has all been sorted out. You will see her later today, I think. Hassan and some others are on their way to the town. His squad has been relocated here. Between us, Jamilla, I suggested this to my husband. He is such a great man; so understanding. He agreed it might be best for everyone. But don't worry. Nothing to worry about at all. I will arrange for Ameena to share this room with you. She will need someone to take care of her for a few days, I guess."

Then Hejjiye got up to go. At the door she turned and said, shaking her head sagely, "Rumours. Never trust in rumours, Jamilla. Remember that."

***

The day was hot. A trace of summer was in the sunshine. Sometime after the noon namaz, one of Hejjiye's storekeeping women brought a bedroll and a pillow and sheets to be put on the extra bed in my room. An hour later, during a pause in which I, and my group, were tearing up clean worn sheets into strips, rolled together and pinned, in order to be used as bandages somewhere else (such tasks had increased in recent weeks), I heard the sound of engines outside the gate. The metal door opened with its usual metallic protest and, for once disregarding decorum, I ran down the four steps of the building and into the courtyard. The flock of pigeons that still nested in nooks and corners of the building fluttered up and resettled again on the sandy ground of the courtyard as I ran to the gate.

The first person to enter was an old woman, walking straight but with the support of a stout walking stick. The stick had a metal ball instead of a handle on top, so that it resembled a club. She pushed away her face cover immediately on entering the courtyard; she had a square, strong, weather-beaten face and wore a silver ring through her right nostril. Three other women, only a bit younger than the first one, followed; Ameena was supported by two of them. She smiled wanly at me, as we exchanged the usual greetings. She did not look injured, though she often winced as the women helped her to my room. But before that, on the veranda, where Hejjiye received this new group, there was a small performance of welcome for the old woman with the metal-balled walking stick, who appeared to be in charge.

Hejjiye went up to her first, which indicated that the old woman was a person of prestige. In the common Arab way—hospitality had to be offered profusely—she said to the old woman that we were honoured to have guests, and especially her as our guest. "Who wouldn't be honoured to have in her house the woman we all love and honour as Umm Layth?" continued Hejjiye in a rhetorical mode.

I could see from the faces of some of the girls and women, who had gathered around, that Umm Layth was a known and revered name. The old woman did not make much of the welcome and, thanking Hejjiye, insisted on walking with Ameena to my room.

***

As soon as Umm Layth and Ameena were in the room, I posed the question that was searing my mind: "What happened?"

Ameena sat down with a sigh on the bed prepared for her.

Umm Layth, who spoke a dialect of Arabic that I was not used to, asked me to close the door. I did so. Then Umm Layth said to Ameena, "Show her, daughter."

She helped Ameena take off her veil and then she pulled up the loose blouse Ameena was wearing. Ameena's back was scarred in strips, as if lashed. It had been dressed, but some of the scars were still bleeding. I was not prepared for this. I started crying.

Umm Layth restored Ameena's dress and turned to me.

"I have heard much of you, daughter," she said, "Your sister here has told me how both of you left your friends and families to fight for us and for the faith. Surely, there is much reward for you and your sister in the hereafter. That I feel in my heart. No, I know it in my heart, for this is the heart of an old woman who has buried a husband and two sons, and prays every day to the Almighty not to have to bury yet another son. Surely, Allah, who is always righteous and merciful, will reward you in His world. Let not this world of imperfect men and small accidents shake your faith in that one truth."

Then, grabbing her knobbed stick and getting up with some effort, she left the room.

***

What happened? That is what I had asked Ameena. But it was a question that was easier to ask than to answer. It took me days before I could piece together an answer. What had happened to leave a burning bush of scars on the back of my friend? How? Why? When?

JIHADI BRIDE

After her marriage ceremony at the orphanage, Hassan took Ameena to a hotel in the Town (there were two still running, and one had been renovated—with funding from a rich Saudi well-wisher, we were told—for use by jihadis), where they spent two nights together. It was paid for by Daesh, as Hejjiye immediately posted. She wrote "the Caliphate." The story was then picked up and turned into a news item by the *Sun,* which reported how ISIS had given a "bonus" of a thousand dollars to a jihadi fighter for his "honeymoon." We derided that word: "honeymoon." Not one of us would have used it. Hassan and Ameena would have been scandalised by the notion that our beloved Caliphate had encouraged something so Western as a honeymoon!

The second morning after his "honeymoon," with their bridal bedsheet stained with the artificial blood of the made-in-China hymen, Hassan started out for the village where he was posted. Ameena realised that she had company in the Mazda SUV, its windows curtained, that Hassan had organised for the journey. One of the women was like her, newly married to a man in Hassan's group, and the other one was going to join her husband. They had no English and spoke a regional Arabic that Ameena barely understood.

Hassan also had a pickup van, mounted with a machine gun. He had eight other men. They set off early in the morning. Hassan, two men with him at the front, drove their

SUV, talking to Ameena in English once in a while. For a while it seemed to Ameena to be the idyll she had not dared to fully imagine, even maybe a version of the *Bonnie and Clyde* world that Michelle, the green-eyed Parisian beauty, might have prayed for. Hassan was very courteous, and he seemed to want to explain the nature of his work to Ameena. He obviously enjoyed speaking English to her as well, and sometimes asked her about an unusual word or its correct pronunciation. He showed a surprising interest in and knowledge of Western fashion brands.

Soon after leaving the town, the landscape changed and the road got narrower and more uneven. By the afternoon, they were driving over a stretch of gravel and hard sand. The sun was harsher. A village appeared at a distance, glimmering against the blank blue sky, shimmering in the heat as if it was a mirage. Hassan's convoy struck off the road and took a narrow path toward the village. "A small detour," Hassan announced. Peering out of the curtains of the Mazda SUV, the other two women drowsing next to her, Ameena could vaguely make out black flags in the village now. It appeared to be a meagre place, and she wondered why Hassan had been instructed to take this detour. She asked him in English. He explained that he had a good friend, another jihadi officer, in the area who had asked him for advice and help. "He saved my life once," Hassan added. "He took a bullet for me."

The sand was hard enough in this stretch for Hassan to instruct the drivers to take the vehicles down the scree and park in the slight shade thrown by it. The area contained only a few trees, and irruptions of caper and acacia bushes. Hassan spoke on his walkie-talkie. They waited.

Hassan posted a few lookouts, though this was well before the American coalition started bombing Daesh, so there was little fear of a sudden attack. The rest of his men drew off to a clump of palm trees, lit a portable oil stove, and started brewing coffee. That is where Hassan's friend joined them.

Hassan's friend was an older man, with a short, almost white beard; he drove over to Hassan's convoy in an ordinary car, a white Volkswagen, with just one of his men in attendance. Something about the friend's bearing made Ameena think that he had been an army officer once. Ameena could watch and hear them talk through the gaps in the curtains on the windows of the Mazda SUV. At first it looked like he had just come over to have coffee with them. But he hadn't. Ameena knew—Hassan had mentioned, not without the residue of a boast, that he had been instructed by "headquarters" to help his friend.

Since all three women had nothing to do but eavesdrop from inside the curtained SUV, Ameena soon gathered the reason for the instructions. Hassan's friend was at the head of a small squad of Daesh fighters quartered in this village. It was not a place of any strategic importance, and the Sunni tribes in the region were generally considered trustworthy, if only because they distrusted Baghdad and the Shia militia far more than they would distrust the Sunni men of Daesh. And yet a problem had cropped up.

"Shia or Kurd family?" asked Hassan. His questions were often answers. But this time he was wrong.

"No, there are none of those in these villages anymore. They fled a long time back. These people are Sunni. They are Bedouin. Rashidi." Judging from the standard Arabic he spoke, was from a city—like Hassan. It enabled Ameena to understand the gist of their conversation. The various Arabic dialects were still impenetrable to her.

"In these parts? Settled in the village? That is strange."

"Not that strange any longer, Hassan," his friend said, "You know the Bedouin have settled down in many places; most of them are nothing more than seminomadic now."

"But Rashidi? They are far from their usual haunts."

Hassan's friend conceded that, but he added that a clan of Rashidi—two or three families, not more, he guessed—had bought some land and settled down in this village a generation ago. Who knows how or why? The old ways had disappeared so quickly within the last three generations, and even groups from the oldest tribes had adjusted in unexpected ways.

"They are basically farmers now. Still breed some camels, but that is it."

"So, what is the problem?" Hassan asked his friend.

"They have a man they won't turn over to us."

"What sort of man?"

"A soldier from the regime, according to the guy who informed on them. A village guy. Greedy—he probably has an eye on their fields. Evidently, there was a soldier who came to this Rashidi clan with a bullet wound, months ago, and they have been hiding him since then."

"Is it confirmed?"

"The head of the clan does not deny it."

"He doesn't! So, what is the problem? Get that government turncoat and shoot the faithless jackal in the village square. No, behead him."

"They won't allow it."

"Who won't allow it?"

"The men of that Rashidi clan. Or their head. Old man. Rheumy eyes, carries an old dagger and an Enfield M1917. From the Second World War, he says very proudly. Can hardly stand straight but his mind is all there. Character from a book; you should see him …"

"I would be tempted to shoot him on the spot!"

Hassan's friend made a wry face and continued: "Anyway, the old fool says the wounded soldier had sought their protection and they cannot turn him over to anyone else, unless he decides to leave of his own free will."

Hassan laughed, disbelievingly. "Are you serious?"

His friend shook his head in affirmation.

Hassan laughed even more loudly, slapping his thigh: "Are these Rashidi serious?"

"Unfortunately, my friend."

"Did you point out to them that we have machine guns?"

"I listed our weaponry to him. I showed him around, too. He looked very impressed, leaning on his Enfield M1917 for support at times."

"So?"

"Nothing."

"Nothing?"

"Nothing. I spelled it out to him and he said, in this dialect I can hardly follow, he said, you wouldn't believe it, he said: 'What wound is deeper than honour lost? What weapon is greater than Allah?'"

"He is one of these old blasphemers who crop up all the time. Ignorant tribals, who have fifty words for a camel but not a word of true faith! Everything they do and say is against Islam; it is almost as if they have taken a vow not to understand the word of Allah!" Hassan exclaimed, "We have to punish them."

"I know, Hassan," his friend argued, "I know and you know, but these illiterate Bedouins, they do not know. This has been their way for centuries. They will walk past an ailing stranger, a dying man, without a second glance, for they trust his life—and their lives—to Allah. If Allah wills, surely the man will live. In this, they have faith like us. But they will not see a Muslim in the man, a Muslim to be helped—they will just see a stranger from an unknown tribe, to whom they owe nothing. Not their concern. They will not offer him their provisions or medicines, which they need to survive themselves, no, not unless he asks for their protection. But if the stranger asks them for their protection, they will kill and die for him—because their honour does not permit them any other recourse."

"They will die for their honour but not for Allah," Hassan scoffed. "Such are the ways of those who love this life more than the life hereafter! They have to be taught a lesson. You know what we believe in, what we fight for, is not this pre-Islamic tribalism. These are fossils from Jahiliyyah! You have to arrest them and execute them."

"Or, my friend," the man suggested, hesitatingly, "If you permit it, we can look the other way and wait. No one needs to know but us. We can wait until this man they are protecting recovers and has to leave them. He cannot live there all his life! Then we will get him—without fighting them."

"No!" thundered Hassan, standing up so suddenly that he knocked a coffee cup over. "No. Never! Those are the compromises that have enabled the infidels to triumph over us for centuries! No. No. No. They have to be punished—it has to be a lesson for others like them in this region. We have to set an example!"

And so it was done. The clan was attacked and overpowered. Their old rifles were no match to the automatic weapons and machine guns of the jihadis. Ameena and the women heard it happen from inside the SUV, which was left where it was with two guards. The firing and blasts lasted for less than thirty minutes. Hassan and his men came back with just one man wounded—a flesh wound through his upper arm. It was almost evening. But they did not leave. There was more to do. They spent the night there. A small area was screened off for the women to relieve themselves; it was the first time Ameena had to use an improvised toilet.

The next morning all the surviving men of the clan—five of them, including a teenager who could not have been more than sixteen—were lined up in the village square. There was no very old man in the group: the clan head Ameena had heard of. He must have been killed in the skirmish. Three of the men were evidently injured. Perhaps one of them was the soldier. Ameena never found out, because she never asked. The women and children of the Rashidi clan were there, too, standing at a distance with the other villagers. All the villagers had been instructed to watch.

Hassan and his convoy drove up. Ameena and the other two women got out of the SUV. Hassan's friend was there, too, but for some reason he entrusted the rest of the action to Hassan, who supervised the execution of the five surviving adult males of the clan. Their crime was announced to the crowd. The glory of God and the eternal righteousness of Daesh were proclaimed. The crowd were instructed to participate in the justice of the Almighty. Then the captured men were lined up against a mud wall and shot by a firing squad in true military style. The shots rang out in a crescendo. There was a second of intense silence, pierced by a slow ululation of sorrow—which had been forbidden by Hassan—from some women in the crowd. Hassan reacted angrily to this, swinging up his M4 automatic, but his friend ignored the matter and instructed his men to clear the area.

It set an example, as Hassan put it.

***

Hassan brought Ameena to a colonial-style bungalow, its white façade pockmarked with bullet holes, in a small Iraqi town whose name, at least at the start, no one would divulge to her. There had once been a garden, and some bushes of Jericho rose had colonised the remnants of the beds, following the recent rains. The bungalow was not very far from the town centre, which had been partly gutted. The town still contained some tawdry shops and a weekly market in which the villagers around the area displayed their steadily diminishing produce and sold poultry.

In the bungalow, divided with curtains and reed mats into a *zenana* section, Ameena met Hassan's earlier wife and his children. Hassan had mentioned his other wife, though not that he had three children from her. Ameena did not make much of that omission. Perhaps he had mentioned it and she had forgotten. She had learned that it is a woman's job to own up to all errors, not to blame them on her husband. (She later discovered that Hassan had yet another wife—and children—safely quartered with his parents in Riyadh.)

Ameena took to her duties with determination. It helped that Hassan's older wife was a villager, devout in a tribal manner that regularly drew Hassan's censure. Closer to Hassan's age, the older wife did not resent Ameena and soon, taking her cue from the children, Ameena started employing the prefix *Umm*—mother—for her. The older woman, in her turn, called Ameena "young wife." In fact, she seemed to welcome Ameena as company, and perhaps as an interpreter to help her sidestep the pitfalls of her flawed and tribal Islam in Hassan's perfect world of Wahhabism. Soon she was trying to improve Ameena's Arabic, while Ameena helped in the education of the children and took over the various religious and social functions that the older wife had been saddled with: organising the women, attending to childbirth and social matters among women, ensuring that the divine word was taught correctly and that necessary political news was circulated among the "weaker sex" too. Hassan's older wife relinquished these activities to Ameena with alacrity, and the suspicion crossed Ameena's mind that Hassan might have been encouraged to marry again by his wife—for, following Islamic precepts, he had asked for and received her permission first—simply in order to be relieved of such chores.

Ameena did not mind them. After all, wasn't she part of a larger cause now? (Why, then, did she feel more lonely than she ever had in her life? Why did she feel more superfluous than she ever had?) Hassan was a sort of deputy governor of the town and he had a full house to himself and his family. He had a couple of women coming in to help with the domestic chores in the zenana section, and a Yazidi boy, not much older than ten, who had been recently captured and sold to Hassan as a slave. His name was Sabah, and he was the only male, apart from Hassan's son and Hassan, who cut across both the men's parts of the house and the zenana section. He was the only male who did chores. Hassan treated Sabah with great disdain: he did not beat him, it is true, but he would often ridicule and humiliate him. For Ameena, however, Sabah soon became a rampart against the tides of loneliness and futility threatening to drown her.

What a flimsy rampart! Sabah was a timid boy, skeletally thin, slightly imbecilic in his gestures, but with delicate features. He seemed frightened to be anywhere near a man, and the words of Hassan would leave his pinched face pale with fear. Ameena soon realised that Sabah acted more like an imbecile when Hassan was around or, from what Hassan told her, in the presence of the other men. Left alone with the women, he behaved normally. It struck Ameena that the imbecility was an act adopted by Sabah to protect himself from the men by providing an easy target for their disdain and feelings of superiority.

It had started in the first week itself when Hassan detained the boy, as he brought a tray of dates into their room in the zenana section.

"Should we stone Sabah for worshipping the Devil?" Hassan said musingly, gripping the boy hard by an arm.

Sabah winced and pretended he did not understand, grinning foolishly. Ameena had not known what to reply.

Hassan continued: "How would you like it, Sabah, you idolater, if we stoned you like your people stoned and killed Du'a Khalil? Do you know she was stoned for marrying a Muslim, you idiot?"

"How would this little boy know?" Ameena expostulated. "It must have been decades before he was born." She did not know what Hassan was talking about, but it sounded like something from a long time back.

"Oh no, no, no," Hassan laughed, "It was in 2007 or 2008. This spawn of a serpent would have been running about around then."

"Crawling about, more likely," Ameena laughed, and somehow Hassan was diverted by the rejoinder.

"Show us how you crawl, Yazidi," he ordered, "Down on all fours and crawl out of my sight."

Sabah obliged with alacrity in his usual imbecilic way. Ameena almost protested, but something in the look on Hassan's face told her that it would be a costly mistake. She was learning fast.

**

Was Sabah Yazidi? Ameena was not sure. Hassan said he was, but Sabah had been with the family for months before Ameena arrived, and the main drive against the Yazidi, which forced them to hide in the mountains of Sinjar, had not started that far back. Or so Ameena estimated. Ameena asked Sabah but the boy did not know, and in any case he spoke a strange language, which sounded only partly Arabic to her ears, and of which Ameena, with her limited, copy-book Arabic, could understand only a few words.

That Hassan considered the boy Yazidi was indubitable, and soon Ameena realised that what really mattered was what Hassan, and people like Hassan, thought. He would, for instance, get his oldest child, a boy of eleven, to cane Sabah whenever Hassan ordered that the slave be punished. Neither Hassan's older wife nor Hassan's son liked being called upon to do so, but neither of them protested. The first time Ameena witnessed this ritual, enforced in person by Hassan, she was ready to go out and protest—she was in the kitchen—but her co-wife held her back and begged her not to do so.

"It would be worse for everyone—for you, for us, for Sabah," she whispered, holding Ameena back.

Later, when the event was over and Sabah had been sent back, snuffling, to the zenana section, Hassan's older wife said to Ameena, in a way that was half-apology, half-warning: "You are an educated woman; I am not. But believe me, young wife, such matters are beyond the understanding of us women. Allah did not make us to understand such things. They are best left to Allah and men."

***

Hassan's wife had eased Ameena's life in many little ways. Looking back, Ameena realised that her natural rebellious-ness would have landed her in trouble with Hassan, who brooked no contradiction from women or juniors, had his older wife not been there. She even treated Ameena's book-ish knowledge of Islam with respect. Hassan on the other hand cared little about the texts that Ameena read—if he had read about Islam once, he had long since ceased to do so, and now he basically went by whatever his group said or practised. His was almost a technological Islam, its pruned rituals as shorn of ambiguity as a hammer or a computer code, Ameena realised. It was a do-it-yourself manual—and he had many of those, too, on repairing motorcycles, pre-paring bombs, assembling guns, electricity, carpentry.... They were all short, concise, to the point, concerned not with theory but with application, not with thought but with practice. Hassan's Islam was a do-it-yourself manual for ... for what? Ameena did not know: It was either for living a certain kind of life or for gaining a certain kind of death, or perhaps both. What she did know was that Hassan did not have any respect for Ameena's scholarly reading of Islam.

On the only occasion when Ameena teased him about an Islamic precept, one she thought he did not really understand, Hassan got out of their bed in irritation and fetched his scoped rifle. He put it in Ameena's lap and said to her, in English, "This is all I need to know about Islam. That is what you whitewashed Muslims have forgotten, and that is why we have had our asses kicked for centuries now."

***

Soon afterward, Hassan and his squad were deputed to administer and control a rural district not far from Tikrit. He had been given the post by the "caliph" himself, it was said. The family, with Sabah, who had by then taken to staying fearfully in Ameena's vicinity when he could, went with him. They relocated, with some other women, in a sprawling rural house, with a courtyard and even a dry, covered well in the kitchen.

But when the Iraqi government forces and Shia militia started winning again, late in November 2014, Hassan sent his older wife and children back to her people across the Syrian border. He trusted the Iraqis much less than the Syrians. Hassan asked Ameena to go too, but Ameena pleaded that, as the youngest and as yet childless bride of a jihadi, it was her duty to stay with Hassan. She knew she was lying. By then Hassan was no longer her reason to be there. She had not been appalled by the brutal punishments that Hassan meted out to suspected traitors and those who disobeyed him; she thought the whippings and beheadings could have been required by the circumstances. She did not know enough to judge. But she could not help noticing the gratuitous violence that Hassan practised under the cloak of his Islam. He would personally behead any traitor, and order all the families—including his own—to witness the beheading. He would cane any child above ten who refused to look upon such public punishments. Given the choice between a lesser punishment and a greater one, he inevitably chose the more gory option. Ameena realised that he looked truly happy only when he left an execution, wiping the sword on his fatigues, his face splattered with blood.

No, Hassan was no longer her reason to stay. It was Sabah. She was afraid of what would happen to this scared, effeminate-looking boy in her absence. He now glanced at her with dumb entreaty whenever Hassan walked into the room, as if imploring her to hide him. She still understood only a few words of his dialect, but they did not need language to communicate. When she could, she found reasons to send Sabah away from Hassan's presence. Ameena was learning to curb her instinct to oppose and criticise—and I wonder now if she noticed the irony of it all: how she had left a world in order to rebel, to fight for what she considered right, and now, now…. In the midst of the ruins in which she had landed—not just the ruins of houses but also the ruin of humanity—Sabah was a symbol of hope. She started thinking of him as a son or younger brother. She could not abandon him to Hassan's mercy, for he was Hassan's slave, and there was nothing anyone could do to change that. She had grown to dread Hassan's moods—his shouting and ranting at everything from presumed traitors to the faithlessness of the villagers to a badly prepared meal in his home had increased as the first rumours, strongly denied, of defeats started trickling in—and she could not abandon this boy, who had even more reasons than her to dread Hassan.

Ameena stayed behind, in a house containing some other wives and mothers of jihadis who had nowhere else to go; she had a whole section of the house to herself, while the other women made do with the rest.

***

A final reason was not long in coming. By December, the Sinjar offensive had soured. The US-led coalition had started its bombing campaigns; often they heard warplanes but they had not been bombed yet, perhaps because the area governed by Hassan had no oil well or strategic significance. But soon, Hassan was informed that a group he had sent to the Sinjar siege—one of his two armoured personnel carriers (an American M113 APC) and seven of his men—had been destroyed in a strike. The message came on his walkie-talkie when he was having a rare meal in the kitchen with Ameena. Only Sabah, who was serving, and Ameena were around.

The news threw Hassan into a fury. He was not too concerned about the men he had lost—for most of the men he had sent were those he dubbed "pillheads" in talking to Ameena. Hassan used "pillheads," in English, to refer to those of his men who took capsules of Captagon before going into battle. Evidently, *real* men needed nothing but their faith in order to murder and rape. Not only did Hassan think lowly of such pillheads, he also knew that, after a certain point, these men became addicted beyond redemption. They could only be used as suicide bombers then. It was the loss of his *American* M113 APC that threw him into a raving fury. He smashed his plate on the floor. He went for Sabah and shook him by the neck. Then, relinquishing the boy suddenly, Hassan stalked out of the kitchen and into the men's section of the house. Sabah fell to the floor and lay there inertly, whimpering in fear until Ameena squatted down beside him and stroked his forehead. The boy put his head in Ameena's lap and closed his eyes. They stayed like that until they heard Hassan coming back, and then they started cleaning up the mess.

Hassan ignored them. He picked up his automatic from the corner where he had forgotten it, and stalked out again. She heard him shout to his men outside. They heard his jeep driving off.

***

But the next night Hassan had news for Ameena. He was going to set an example. He had discussed it with his advisors and cleared it with his superiors too: they were going to execute all the "Devil-worshippers" in the village. They were going to film the execution and put it on YouTube. He would behead them personally, and he would warn the crusading armies of Rome that for every jihadi they killed, he would behead as many infidels. "Come and face the wrath of God," he shrieked, fists raised, sitting up suddenly in bed. "Come and face the wrath of God!"

Ameena thought it was just one of his usual rants. Then the term "Devil-worshippers" came back to her. Devil-worshippers in this part of the world? She knew that the Yazidis were considered Shaitan-worshippers by both religious Christians and religious Muslims, but there were no Yazidis in this region. What did Hassan mean?

"Are there Devil-worshippers here?" she asked. She found herself on slippery grounds when she spoke her pidgin Arabic, but she had realised that Hassan expected her to eschew English, unless he wanted to speak it himself.

"Of course. Sabah in our own house!"

"But," Ameena protested, "You know that Sabah says the fatiha. He has converted to Islam. I have been teaching him."

Hassan laughed. "Sure," he said, "To save his skin. Once an idolater, always an idolater."

Ameena was not willing to give up that easily. She had read her Islamic texts with great diligence. "But that is not what my Islam says," she protested, "We cannot kill any innocent person and certainly not one who claims to be a Muslim."

Hassan got out of bed.

"Please get up," he said to Ameena, courteously. In English.

Ameena got up, flustered and confused. As soon as she was on her feet, Hassan slapped her hard, sending her flying back on to the bed, her nose bleeding.

"That will teach you to talk back to your husband and to harbour the germ of doubt," said Hassan calmly, as he left the room.

It was the first time anyone had hit Ameena.

***

Hassan was gone the next day and night. This was not un-usual. He took the precaution of sleeping in different places on different nights. When he returned to the house, he found Ameena worried. She said that she had been trying to contact him and had told the women to get news across to him—they were not allowed to use any electronic means to communicate with any of the fighters anymore, because the Americans were said to be monitoring everything. Hadn't he heard? No, he hadn't. What was the matter?

"Sabah," Ameena gasped. "Sabah ran away yesterday."

Hassan laughed. "Ran away? That moron? Where will he run away? He cannot run anywhere without being spotted."

"Who knows," Ameena replied, "I have looked everywhere; I have had the women look. No one has seen or heard of him since yesterday."

"We will find him," said Hassan, unperturbed. "He must have been sneaking around and overheard what I said to you. He thinks he can hide his pumpkin head away. Where can he go? We will find him and, by God, we need him now. Don't we need him, the devious Yazidi! We need his pumpkin head."

He chuckled, as if at a private joke.

Then he suddenly peered with suspicion at Ameena, his eyebrows beetling: "Are you sure you haven't tucked him away in some cupboard?" he asked.

"Where? Is there an empty cupboard in this house?" Ameena laughed stiffly, "And would I tell you that he was missing if I had anything to do with it?"

"One of the other women would have told me in any case. Or I would have found out when I called for him," Hassan replied.

"I would have to be crazy to hide him," Ameena said, "Why should I even want to do so?"

"Yes," Hassan agreed, "You would have to be crazy to hide him. We are the eyes of Allah."

***

But more than a week went by and no one could find Sabah. Hassan stopped doing other things and, taking a bunch of his men with him, went combing the suspicious houses, one by one, obsessed with finding the slave boy. Some people were slapped around; women were threatened. It did not help. There was no trace of Sabah. He seemed to have disappeared into thin air, and some of the more credulous village women started whispering about the black magic known to these Devil-worshippers. This infuriated Hassan further: though he was willing to kill Sabah for being a "Shaitan-worshipper," his textual, urban Islam did not permit him to give credence to such superstitions as "black magic."

Hassan would still return to the house some nights, usually when he wanted sex, and Ameena would make herself available to him, mechanically, as she always had, even at the beginning. It must have struck her (for Ameena was always the thinker, more than I was in those days) that what she did for her religion with Hassan now was not very different from what she did when, a promiscuous young girl, she had made herself available to young boys from school or her neighbourhood—in order to be considered cool, not religious, during that period. Sometimes, after the act, Hassan would leave and look for Sabah even at night, somehow believing that the boy might come out from his hiding place in the dark. Weeks passed; the chill of the winter nights started being diluted by the gathering warmth of the days. Once Ameena tried to convince him that Sabah must be far from the place by now, but Hassan laughed at the suggestion. "No, he would have been spotted," he said.

"The boy is hiding somewhere. He has been hidden by some family. How would he survive if no one was hiding him?"

Then, suddenly, he looked at Ameena and said, "Are you sure you do not know where he is?" And he laughed a hard laugh.

The next day Hassan sent two of his men to search his own house, ordering the women and Ameena into a bare room in the meantime. The men opened all the cupboards and looked under every bed. They left the house in a greater mess than it was in, but they did not discover Sabah.

After this, Ameena tried not to mention Sabah at all. She redoubled her efforts to be a good wife. She became very good at being a proper Islamic wife, even by Hassan's exacting standards of servitude.

***

Sabah was discovered by a fluke. The village was finally bombed. Their house was spared, but one freak bomb landed on the kitchen, destroying most of it and killing a woman who was there. Some jihadis were killed, too, elsewhere in the village. Hassan and his men were too busy with their own ranks and losses to help with the kitchen until much later in the day, but then, cleaning up the rubble, they heard the sound of moaning from the covered, dry well. Removing the metal lid, they peered in and discovered that some bricks had fallen loose from the sides of the well, partly burying a boy. The boy was still alive, though. It was Sabah.

Sabah was pulled out of the rubble and the well. Despite scratches and cuts, he could walk. He was taken to Hassan and interrogated. It was obvious to anyone that Sabah could not have descended down the well—and put the metal lid back on—without an adult's help. Moreover, he had hidden there for weeks: someone must have been sneaking food to him. Who was this traitor?

***

It was then that Ameena went to the oldest woman in the house and confessed to her in broken Arabic. Ameena knew Hassan would guess, and he would definitely torture Sabah to extract a confession. She confessed to the older woman. Ameena revealed that she had hidden Sabah in the well; she had sneaked food, blankets, and water to him. She had even drawn up his refuse bucket and disposed of its contents, on nights when she could.

"Why, daughter? Why did you do such a foolish thing?" the older woman asked. She must have been eighty. She had only a few teeth left but was still fully alert, and walked almost straight, with the aid of a metal knobbed walking stick. She was held in much esteem by the jihadis because her husband and two of her sons had been "martyred," and some of her other sons and their sons were known to be fighting against the Shia government of Iraq. In the house, they called her Umm Layth, though Ameena understood this was not her name but an honorific bestowed on her: she was the "mother of lions."

Umm Layth looked at Ameena with yellow eyes, dull but shrewd. Ameena knew that she could not tell her how, despite her faith, she found the treatment of Sabah unacceptable, how she believed that the Prophet, blessed be his name, had preached against slavery, that he had accepted it but indicated that it should be discouraged, urging people to free their slaves if they could, insisting on rights for slaves, and ensuring that the first call to prayer was sounded by a black ex-slave. Would Umm Layth understand all this? Would she wish to understand it? If she understood it, would she even want to bring it up with the men? And, in any case, if she did, would it make any difference?

No, Ameena knew by now that it would not. (Am I the only one who sees the tragedy in this, or do you too: the morphing of Ameena, the bold rebel, into Ameena, the duplicitous liar?) Truth and rebellion were not possible for her; not even the truths of Islam, as she understood them. The fault would have to be hers; no, the fault was hers; there was something deficient in her understanding of Islam, some virus of Western contamination, surely!

She said to Umm Layth: "Sabah reminded me of the son I do not have, Mother. I was weak. I am a weak woman."

Umm Layth shook her white head pityingly.

"Surely you will have many sons, daughter," she said, "Hassan will give you many sons; keep your trust in Allah's beneficence. Your sons will be lions; they will roar for righteousness, and this world of iniquities will tremble at their voice."

But it must have been Umm Layth who ensured that when the village mullahs were asked to judge Ameena, her crime was seen as a woman's weakness and not as a matter of faith and doubt—for which the punishment would have been much harsher. Instead, she was sentenced to just ten lashes in one public session. Though there was no expectation that he should, Hassan volunteered, with the necessary words of piety, to take upon himself the duty of chastening his errant wife and administering the punishment. It was only proper. You see, a woman could not administer the punishment, not properly, for women are weak, and neither could a man not related to Ameena, without dishonouring Hassan.

THE SOUNDS OF WAR

I stroked Ameena's forehead. She could not yet lie on her back. At night I had to ensure—as Umm Layth had instructed me—that Ameena was gently turned to lie on her sides, because if she lay flat in her sleep she would wake up in pain. It took two or three more weeks for Ameena to heal fully, during which Umm Layth and her three decrepit old women were the only people visiting her and administering balms. Hejjiye inquired after her from me but did not visit the room. Hassan, of course, could not come into our room or section, and Ameena was in no condition to be taken out to wherever he was quartered, or so Umm Layth maintained, and I sometimes suspected that the sharp old woman had arranged for Ameena to be moved in with me simply in order to keep her from Hassan.

Gathering the story, some bits from Umm Layth, some from Ameena, I finally asked Ameena one day, because the thought had been driving sleep from my eyes, "What happened to the boy, to Sabah?"

By then Ameena's back was almost healed. We were sitting up, having coffee, which was rare—as coffee was getting impossible to obtain. But some victory had recently been announced and extra sugar and coffee had been distributed in celebration.

Ameena did not look up from her cup. She had become very guarded in her responses, speaking much less and more carefully than she used to in England. She spoke more like a book now, like Mrs. Chatterji, slipping only slightly into the accents of her childhood English.

"Yer see, Jamilla," she replied in English, "Allah always has a purpose; he is kind to us even in our errors."

She sipped from her cup, holding it between palms, as if it was a bowl—maybe it lacked a handle; I do not recall—and continued: "A wor unconscious for almost a day after Hassan finished lashing me. He didn't stint. No, he didn't. Hassan never stints in matters of faith. And why should he? He's a true believer and A deserved to be punished. A wor unconscious for a day an' delirious for two or three other days. It wor in that period they beheaded Sabah. It wor public of course; all of us were required to witness it. But A wor delirious; A couldn't be taken anywhere. Yer see what A mean: Allah is merciful."

Did Ameena really think so, I wondered? Did she really consider it an act of mercy? Or had she bought Hassan's version of the faith to such an extent that she did not even feel, as I felt deep in my heart, that it was all wrong, that no religion could justify such things, and if it did, then, surely, there cannot be a God. To continue to be a believing Muslim—as I was, as I still am—one had to refuse the Islam of the Hassans and Hejjiyes of the world. It was clear to me then. Couldn't Ameena, always more intellectual, always more rebellious than me, see that?

But I could not say it to her. There was a wall of caution, if not suspicion, between me and everyone else now. I could not say it to anyone there. I doubted that I could have said something like that even to my brother and father in England, had I realised this earlier on. I doubt people like them would be willing to listen even today, and that is one reason—by no means the only one—why I am talking to you here in Bali, and not somewhere in England. Can I go back and live with people who love me and whom I love, but who will refuse to countenance this scalding fact? Can I go back and keep my faith among people, my own family members, who reduce God to a little bookkeeping clerk, who commit the blasphemy—for what greater blasphemy can there be if you believe in God?—of claiming to know the mind of God, of speaking in his voice, of insisting on their fallible, human interpretations of his Word? But I do not want to bother you with my thoughts; let me return to the facts of my story.

***

In the fortnight that Ameena was recovering in my room, Hejjiye called for a purge of books. She went through the small library—already with many bare shelves—that we had and pulled out a stack of books. Some of them were by orthodox Islamic scholars whom I had read and who had been quoted favourably in the past—but they had evidently fallen out of favour with Daesh now. We were instructed to pile the tomes in the centre of the courtyard, and to be fully veiled as the men in the guardhouses outside were called in to supervise the bonfire. Hejjiye had me film all of it using her iPhone. I knew she would post it online later: the sight of women, hooded in niqabs, setting fire to a pile of books while chanting "Allah is Great" was her little contribution to the cause. The bearded men were probably there for greater effect; Hejjiye knew how to offend the West. My short film would, I knew, circulate in the West and cause some bitterness and much unease. Hejjiye's belief in its justice had stayed unwavering all these months, and in my bitter moments I wondered whether it was because of real faith or just convenience, the convenience of power and prestige that it provided her with. It was a thought I would not even express fully to myself, let alone to Ameena or anyone else. The freedom from conscription into alien ways that I had sought in England had led to this!

The sight of the books burning inevitably called back to my mind the memory of the only time that James had violently disagreed with Ameena and me. This was after the Alex matter, when I had patched up with Ameena and we had again become the best of friends. Once again, the inadvertent initiator of the controversy was Mrs. Chatterji, in her literature class. This time the assignment was "literary controversies." It was meant to be a group project. James was in our group, along with another girl, a Muslim, though not as religious as me or Ameena, whose parents were from Algeria or Tunisia, I forget which. We chose to work on the controversy around Salman Rushdie.

Neither I nor Ameena had read *The Satanic Verses* and we had no intention of doing so. The other girl dabbled in it, found it boring or confusing, and desisted after a few dozen pages. James continued gamely, professing bewilderment at times, and trying to sound us out about Islamic notions of blasphemy. But Ameena and I were not in the mood to engage with *The Satanic Verses*; we had not chosen Rushdie in order to read that novel but to use the controversy to highlight what we considered the duplicity of the West. We had our arguments in place, having heard them rehearsed many times by people who, like us, never had and never would read the novel: how European nations, including

England, still had blasphemy laws and how they only covered Christianity, how England had banned books left and right in the past both at home and in its colonies, and even if books were not banned today, the nature of commercialisation and other cultural controls ensured their invisibility, how there was a long tradition in the West of denigrating Islam in particular and the beliefs of coloured people in general, and so on. We had a long list. James agreed with some of the criticism and had reservations about some. But we did not fall out over such differences, which James was willing to overlook in the face of our adamant refusal to mitigate the sheer villainy of the West, villainy that stretched in an unremitting line right from the earliest crusades down to Guantanamo in our puritanical view of the vacillating and mutual crimes of history. He had trouble accepting our defence of the fatwa against Rushdie, but he did not argue with us about that. What he could not accept was our defence of the book burning associated with the protests. We justified it; he wanted nothing but a clear rejection of any kind of book burning. Our argument was heated, with the Tunisian or Algerian girl trying to support James without offending us and being accused of not being really Muslim.

Finally, James burst out, addressing me in particular, "How can yer, Jamilla—yer take such good care of the 'oly Quran, yer even 'andle the Bible with respect, how can yer call for burning a book?"

"But James," I scoffed in a superior tone, "Surely you are not equating a filthy little novel with revealed texts?"

"They are all books," he maintained.

"Burning a novel is not the same as burning a book of revelation!"

"'Tis," James maintained, his face getting redder than usual. "Burning a book's like burning a human being. Once yer start burning books, yer end up burning the entire world, every damn human being in it!"

We never resolved that difference, and had to leave references to book burning out of our project report. At that moment, Ameena and I were angry at James for being so obdurate: he had revealed, we later told each other, his true colonial colours, for had he not implied that there was something barbaric about the way in which religious Muslims had protested against Rushdie's novel? And what a melodramatic conclusion: "Once you start burning books, you end up burning the entire world, every damn human being in it!" James, truly!

Now, watching the books burn in Hejjiye's orphanage, making the pigeons flap around in consternation for the first time, I thought of James and was surprised to realise that I understood his frustration—was it because at least some of the books were commentaries on the Quran by people I had read and whose views I had believed in? Suddenly, these people were no longer to be read because they had criticised Daesh! How many more will join the pyre over the next few months, I wondered. I could see what James had meant when he pronounced that once you start burning books you end up burning the entire world.

As Ameena was still recovering, she had been excused by Hejjiye—on Umm Layth's suggestion—from attending the "purification" ceremony. When I returned to her room, she asked me what had happened. I described the scene to her. I could not tell her exactly what I thought. Caution had become second nature with us. But then, I could not help adding, "Remember James? Remember the argument we had over burning books?"

She nodded.

"As I saw the books burn, I could almost hear him shout at us. For a moment, I thought I saw him."

"James, there? Now that would be something," Ameena said.

I think the same image might have crossed our minds at that instant—large, amoebic, red-faced James, always striving to see the other person's perspective, in that blinkered crowd of bearded men and hooded women. The incongruity of it struck us at the same time, and we started giggling uncontrollably. We could not laugh openly; laughing openly was considered un-Islamic by some. We giggled uncontrollably, muffling our faces, until some involuntary movement hurt Ameena and she gasped with the pain. When she recovered, she looked at me as she used to, oh, so long ago, before Hassan, before, maybe even before Istanbul, and she said, "You would not mind arguing with James once again, would you, Jamilla?"

At that moment, I felt that Ameena understood me, after all, and perhaps shared my doubts, my unease. But she did not allow me the time to respond. She coughed, as if in embarrassment, as if ashamed, and added, "No, no, forget I said that. Forget it."

***

That was the last time I saw Ameena laugh aloud. Have you noticed this about Islamists? I do now: They find it so difficult to smile. (Some of Hejjiye's chaperones would scold those orphans who laughed loudly.) Is it because they take themselves too seriously? Is it because they think of God as an unsmiling old man, despite the fact that their Islam prohibits them from assigning any shape or form to Allah? Or is it just a culture of obedience and respect that has to be ingrained in children by adults? I guess these and other explanations are all valid. But whatever the explanations, once Ameena healed and rejoined our normal activities, she adopted that stern, unsmiling attitude. If she had to smile, she pursed her lips, as if she was repressing a distasteful impulse, and what appeared on her face was more a grimace than a smile.

I have remarked about her eyes, haven't I? How she had these limpid eyes, with depths in them, as if they were dark pools of light in which lurked the deeper shadow of a hurt? I have said how the light had hardened into anger over the years? But now when I looked at her, I felt that the light had been switched off, the pools had dried. There was just a brittle layer of silt left in them.

More and more, Ameena secluded herself from others—especially me—and took to reading religious texts in her spare time. She also volunteered for whatever chore or activity might take Hejjiye's fancy. It took me a few weeks to concede to myself that something had broken in Ameena: she was no longer the spunky girl I had met in our school-yard. For the first time I wondered if, given that choice, I would still approach the old Ameena, pulling ferociously at a cig behind the playground slide, and hector her about the unsuitability of her habit. I realised with a shock that I missed the old Ameena, and with her, I missed people like James. But I pushed the thought away.

Then, as Ameena took to currying favour with Hejjiye and her people, I suspected that perhaps "broken" was not the right word for Ameena. Something had changed, but it seemed to be a determined change. Ameena had set out to become another Hejjiye—even a more austere version of Hejjiye.

I have told you that Hejjiye liked me from the start: she appreciated beautiful, submissive girls, and she enjoyed fixing up their marriages with her husband's jihadi friends. She had once said to me, in the sort of grand-aunt manner that she could slip into as easily as into her other characters (knowing woman-of-the-world, amateur preacher, perfect wife, loving mother, reliable friend, sister, principal, Internet expert, practical Arab housewife, and so on): "Jamilla, you know, you are almost famous in these parts. At least a dozen men want to marry you from what they have heard of you!"

"I have work to do and things to learn here," I had demurred, as always. "It is not time for me to marry. Not before Damascus falls to us, I have vowed to Allah."

"True," she had conceded grudgingly. "And, anyway, we don't want to be without you."

Hejjiye liked having pretty women around her; I suspect it was only the unattractive girls who got talked into becoming suicide bombers. And of course those who had witnessed such violence done to them or theirs that it had burnt up everything in their hearts except the thirst for revenge—merciless revenge in the merciful name of Allah. How did you put it in one of your essays? I read it sometime back: yes, you wrote that violence spreads like a virus by contaminating others. Or something like that. And, great god, there had been an epidemic of violence in those parts.

Jealousy and suspicion spread like viruses too. As Ameena started ingratiating her way into Hejjiye's favour,

I suspect I caught an infection of both. Yes, even jealousy, for though I was cautious with Hejjiye and did not trust her after what had happened to Halide, she was still the sun around which our little world revolved, and to some extent all of us desired to bask in her rays. Now, Ameena slowly worked her way into becoming Hejjiye's favourite. This roused my jealousy and suspicion: was Ameena up to something that might diminish my status, create problems for me? Yes, that is what a claustrophobic world can cause: infections spread faster in confined space.

***

What about Hassan? you ask. He was around, but busy with his manly tasks. He was now just one of the deputy commanders of the region, and his squad was depleted. Maybe it was because of his responsibilities, or maybe it was because of what had happened between him and Ameena, but he never visited her. Other jihadi husbands would visit occasionally and meet their wives in the courtyard—sometimes the wives might go away, too, for a day or more. Actually, more women were leaving than arriving now. The sounds of war were louder. Sometimes, depending on the direction of the wind, we could smell gunpowder or fires: the smell of burning rubber in particular carries a long way. The nights, once so quiet, were regularly shattered by distant explosions; planes and helicopters flew over us every week now, and the town was bombed at least once more.

There were maybe five or six girls left now, as some had departed to join their families while some more had been married off. All the others—more than twenty grown women and children—were related to jihadis. Then, of course, there were those two Kurdish women prisoners. There was even some talk of leaving the place and moving into town, which was better defended than our outlying orphanage, but Hejjiye was against it, because—she argued—the town was being bombed and the orphanage would not be.

***

When Ameena and I had arrived in the orphanage—not even a year ago!—it had seemed strangely different from what we had expected. As I told you, we had seen very little sign of active conflict—the area, leading from Raqqa to this region and beyond, had been firmly under Daesh control. The violence I had heard of since then had been punitive in nature—a version of what happened to Sabah or Ameena elsewhere, I am sure now, but easy for me to ignore, because we mostly got only one-sided reports. We had witnessed bombed buildings, twisted metallic hulks that had once been cars, and cratered roads, but mostly there was a layer of dust on these signs of destruction. Over all of it the black Daesh flag flew, confident and assured. And then the orphanage itself, with its tiled wall, its great gate, its courtyard with pigeons and sparrows; the wide, white building had not borne the mark of even a single bullet. It was, looking back, the perfect place to bring someone like Ameena or me—trophy "Western" jihad-ists—to the cause! But now this was all to change. The dust that had settled on one round of violence and destruction in these parts—a round that had ended a bit before we arrived—was to rise again, as the sun got hotter, the winds blew up the sand in the fields into gusts, and the sound of warfare drew nearer.

With this, the equanimity of the women and girls in the orphanage also disappeared. It could have gone badly for Dilnaz and Sera. Some of the women would have stoned them out of sheer aimless frustration and anger. The men outside, under Hassan, might have raped them. I no longer had any doubt that such rapes were taking place; they were not just rumours and "Western propaganda," as Hejjiye used to put it. Or "misunderstandings." I recall that, once, months ago, when the rape of Shia, Christian, or Yazidi women had blown up on the Internet—this was before our Internet service broke down for good—and become impossible for us to ignore in the orphanage, Hejjiye had arranged for a Daesh-sanctioned imam to speak to us about it. He might have been the last "guest speaker" we had. He was an old man with the blue eyes many Syrians had, ill at ease in a room full of women, despite our total veils, and he had spoken to us as if we were all fifteen years old. He had spoken specifically on the topic, "Western Misinformation about Rape." It was, he had argued, his blue eyes fixed above us, some saliva speckling his salt-and-pepper beard, an "infidel" interpretation of what actually happened: the women had been given into the care of honourable Daesh fighters, either because the women had so wished or to protect them, for a woman without a man was weak and fallible, and surely if a woman, in such circumstances, could not have a husband, she was still safer in the care of an honourable man of the faith, who would satisfy her womanly needs and protect her at the same time?

This lecture was before Ameena's return, soon after Halide's "marriage." It had been difficult, even then, to listen to this convoluted and self-seeking argument, I have to concede that to you. But I had. And so had the others.

Some had surely believed in the bearded old man; some, like me, must have chosen not to disbelieve—for can one really believe if there is no freedom to disbelieve? What is the credit in having faith if you allow others and yourself no real choice at all?

Anyway, the situation had changed now. Most of the women were used to scarcities—for instance, the paucity of water, as our supply broke down. I wasn't; I had grown up taking the water supply for granted. But I had one advantage over the other women. I had stopped believing—or, rather, pretending to myself that I still believed—in the Daesh. It was easy for me to do so (and to keep it hidden). I did not feel I had anything apart from my own belief invested in the people there. I had chosen to join them out of personal conviction; I could still retreat into this small room of belief in myself and ignore them: in some ways, this was no different from how I had grown up and lived in England! That was not the case with most of the women there, especially those who had nowhere else to go. And only those were left now.

Yes, it would have ended badly for Dilnaz and Sera, but for Hejjiye—who needed to ensure the safety of these two captives in order to maintain her own authority—to give them over to Hassan's men outside (if they craved them, which is just my guess) would be to lose whatever control she had, and much of it was simply because she was the main wife of Commander Abu Jalal in town. But would Hejjiye have stopped the women in the orphanage from abusing the captives in anything more than words? Once in a while, when we got bad news, some of the women would rail against the captives, storm to the cell and curse them, spit at them; they would demand that the keys be handed over to them, so that they could punish those "shameless witches." I am afraid Hejjiye might have done less to stop the women on such occasions, had it not been for Umm Layth and her group. Almost every time something like this happened, the old woman would hobble up and stand between the screaming women and the bars of the cell.

Why did she do so, you ask? Truly, I do not know. Umm Layth never spoke kindly of—let alone to—the Kurdish prisoners. She often wished the curse of Allah on them and their families. But she always hobbled up and calmed down the women, insisting that such matters are best left to Allah and to the menfolk.

***

The summer swelled like a fever outside. In the afternoons, the sun was so strong that even the pigeons abandoned our courtyard, seeking the shady corners of the building. The weeks passed. We slowly learned to bracket out the sounds of warfare and to blow out the candles and lamps—or switch off the lights, when there was electricity—if we heard the sound of planes at night. We cooked, cleaned, ground the little grain that we got, cut clothes into bandages, said our prayers—the classes had long disappeared—and encouraged each other to pretend that the tide would turn all of a sudden. There was more talk of us moving into town now.

Having healed, Ameena adopted a meek, submissive persona that, to be honest, I had trouble associating with the girl I recalled from school. She had become even more devout, if that was possible, spending hours on the prayer mat. She took on the most menial tasks and behaved almost like a slave in front of Hejjiye. When she mentioned Hassan during meals or conversations, she spoke of him with admiration and respect. She often seemed to me to be that stereotype of a woman who, as some men are supposed to believe, just "needs a slap or two" to be kept on the straight and narrow. With me, she was very reserved—she even avoided my eyes now, as if she had something to hide—and the only woman with whom she sat on her own, though without talking, was Umm Layth.

Ameena's docility and obvious contrition paid dividends. She gradually replaced me in Hejjiye's esteem. I did not regret it altogether, at least not at the start, as Hejjiye had started putting greater pressure on me to marry a jihadi now. But when Hejjiye told me that I did not need to do my duties at the cell of the Kurdish women, as Ameena was replacing me, I felt so angry at Ameena that I could not speak to her for the rest of the day. But I suppose you are getting an idea of me by now: I was not, I am not, a person who reacts too quickly. I am, as I said, my mother's daughter in that respect.

The war was all around us now. We got into the habit of listening to the sounds of the war as a diversion; the local women would try to guess where they were coming from. "Surely it is village such-and-such to the north of the Town," one would say. "No," another would correct her, "That would be too close. This is at least two miles further off. It is village so-and-so." "Ah, village so-and-so," a third would join the conversation, "One of my daughters was married into that village." There would be concern for her. "Where is your daughter now, may Allah preserve her?" "She is dead; Allah took her away in childbirth a long time ago." There would be muttered commiseration, lines from the Quran.

Another blast would sound and a different woman would offer a guess.

Always the women could tell not just the direction from which the sounds came but also, more or less, the villages in the area. The rest of us, who were from elsewhere, would listen. Despite talk of retreating to the Town, which was getting bombed steadily now, we felt that we were safer in the orphanage than we would be anywhere else.

Then, one night, a bit after midnight, everything changed for good. The sound of firing and the explosions moved much nearer, but more than that, they seemed to come from all directions at the same time. Hejjiye had a hurried conversation over her iPhone—hardly used any longer—and the door in the gate was opened. We were instructed to stay veiled all the time when not in our rooms. We were also told to stay in our wings. Three of Hassan's men came in and occupied Hejjiye's office, which had two windows looking out over the football field and the ruins behind us. We were asked to barricade the windows in our rooms—most of them already shuttered and bolted—with whatever furniture we could smash up or fit in.

Hejjiye moved into our wing, the one with the cell. The firing ended almost as suddenly as it had started—after about two hours—but none of us could sleep that night. Looking back, I can recall that the only person who remained totally unaffected was Ameena. There was even a grim look of satisfaction on her face—and it was only later that the suspicion dawned on me that Ameena had, even then, been envisioning her act of martyrdom, and my involuntary role in it.

***

We should have left then—Hejjiye said a number of times later, when we were marooned in the orphanage, cut off from the town. We should have left that day.

But we didn't. The news was that the Peshmerga offensive had been stalled, and that more jihadi fighters were on their way—that the Peshmerga would be running from our boys soon. It didn't happen. Either the reinforcements did not arrive, or the Kurds preempted the Daesh.

As if it was a repeat performance, at almost the same time as the previous night, there was a terrific explosion. The girls who had fallen asleep woke up screaming. This was the first time that an explosion had made our building shake, the panes and doors rattle. Then, following a pause, we heard the scream of planes—or drones—and two spots in the Town lit up with bombs, again and again. The glare was strong enough to be reflected on our walls. At the same time, there was a burst of gunfire and the rumble of explosions all around us.

Hejjiye ordered us to stay in our rooms. Ameena lay unmoved in her bed. I took to the Quran, my usual resort in moments of crisis. This continued for some time, and then, just as it seemed that we were finally getting used to it, there were a series of thuds. For a moment I thought someone was hammering in a nail somewhere in the building. Then, as, again for the first time, Hassan's men started firing back and we could hear his precious armoured carrier move to the side of the building, I understood the thuds. They were bullets hitting our building.

By dawn, the situation was clear. The Peshmerga had made a sudden pincer movement at night and gained a number of villages. There was a squad of them in the ruins across the football field, and others in buildings on the out-skirts of the town. The jihadi forces had fallen back to the other side of the town. We were basically cut off from them, that is, unless we braved a kilometre or more of open fire to reach the town and then fought through the Kurdish squads on this side of it. It was effectively a siege.

Even though Hejjiye and her women had instructed us not to do so, I could not help sneaking into a room with a window, all of them doubly shuttered and barricaded in the two wings now, but with chinks in it. One could look out through the chinks to the fields behind the building. I could discern that there was a strange flag fluttering in the ruins of the torched Shia houses. Apart from that, everything seemed as it had been. There was no movement anywhere, not even the barrel of a gun poking out. The firing had ceased too, as it almost always did in the early mornings.

But the door on the gate was open now, and Hassan had a couple of men placed, behind a barrier of sandbags, on the roof just above Hejjiye's office. He had a couple of men in the office too. He was running around, swinging his scoped M4 assault rifle to give directions; his magazine carrier now hung with grenades too. The men had monopo-lised the middle section of the building, inducing Hejjiye to move the few girls left in the dormitory wing to our side. We could watch what was happening through a partition of reed mats that had been hung at the entrance of our wing. Even in such an emergency, Hejjiye was not going to forget the rules of her Islam: women had to be segregated from men.

Ameena observed me peering into the chinks and asked me to be careful. "They might shoot at t'windows too," she said, "Our men's been firing from Hejjiye's office." Then she made a rare gesture of affection, reaching out and stroking away a strand of hair from my face. "A've to speak to Hejjiye," she said, and left the room.

At that moment, the firing started again. It came this time from the ruins on the other side. Hassan's men—they had now moved the machine gun to the rooftop—fired back. Nails were being hammered into the building again.

***

The Peshmerga manoeuvre had taken Hassan and his men by surprise. They had not been expecting the Peshmerga forces to move so fast, without even waiting for their heavy guns to arrive. They had taken a risk. If Hassan had more men, or more guns, he could have launched a counterattack and routed them. But Hassan had less than a dozen men, three injured now, and only one mounted machine gun and an armoured carrier. It was not sufficient to take on the Peshmerga forces, and once the Kurdish heavy guns reached their advance forces, it would be a lost battle. The village was cut off from other jihadi lines, and Hassan could not count on immediate relief from any neighbouring commander—no one in the area had men or weapons to spare any longer. From what we gathered, all Daesh and allied units were struggling simply to hold their positions.

Was Hassan worried about us too—the children and women in the building? Yes, he was—but I suspect it was more because of Hejjiye and her children. Maybe Umm Layth, too, as she was almost legendary in the region. But mostly Hejjiye, who was one of the wives of a powerful man, Commander Abu Jalal. She and her children had been entrusted to Hassan's care. His inability to protect them might have repercussions. It would definitely reflect poorly on his capabilities as a leader and a military strategist. It might lose him command and privileges. I am sure Hassan was aware of such worldly factors, too, despite all his talk of jihad and Allah. The careerists win everywhere, believe me! Hassan's fanaticism was a career to him. Killing was his corporate job. Apocalypse was how he planned to corner the market.

***

The electricity had been cut the previous day. There had been no Internet for weeks. Hejjiye was the only person allowed to use a mobile, apart from Hassan and his men, and they were not communicating with us, anyway, except occasionally to ask us for food or water or bandages, which we handed out across the reed mats. It was a slow day. There were no routines anymore. Some cooking was done. The prisoners had been forgotten, and I think they had not been sent a meal since the day before—which they might have welcomed, for it was best to be forgotten in the situation.

But, no, I was wrong. They had not been forgotten. At least Ameena had remembered them. They were going to be the cornerstone of her martyrdom, that desperate last bid, as I thought when the plan was revealed to me, for Ameena to impress whoever it was she wished to impress: Alex, her mother or father, Hassan, Hejjiye? And I, well, I was just a pebble in that grand plan, a small, inconsequential detail.

I learned about the plan after the *asr*, the afternoon prayer. Ameena had been closeted with Hejjiye; then the two, fully veiled of course, had gone out to talk to Hassan in what used to be Hejjiye's office. They had been gone for at least two hours. They had come back in time for the asr prayer, just as the firing ceased. At first I thought the firing had stopped because it was time to say the prayer. I soon realised that this was for other reasons.

I was saying my prayer when Ameena and Hejjiye returned to our wing. By the time I finished, they had started on theirs. But then, as soon as Hejjiye finished—Ameena had finished a minute earlier—she came over to me. I was in the kitchen, helping in the cooking. Umm Layth and some other women were there too.

Hejjiye walked briskly into the large room, its walls stained with cooking, utensils stacked in rows on one side. She always walked briskly. I was slicing onions. They were among the last left in our storeroom. Without even avoiding the onion fumes, she drew me up—we were almost the same height, but she was a broader woman—and embraced me. "What you have decided to do, Jamilla, you and the blessed Ameena, will be recalled among us for generations, yea, for centuries. I just wish I did not have the responsibilities that prevent me, or I would join you here—and in paradise."

What had I decided to do? I had no idea. If there was anything I had decided to do, weeks ago, it was to do just what was necessary to survive and nothing more. To survive with the minimum of doing until some stroke of fortune released me into the wider world outside. I had so often rejected that world for being imperfect, and thus an affront to the perfection of my God, but its human imperfection was exactly what I had grown to respect in this place where all talk of perfection and purity led, by a straight and narrow road, directly to suffering, mistrust, destruction, and death. What, I wondered, could I have decided to do that brought tears of joy into Hejjiye's light brown eyes?

It was revealed to me. Some bits by Hejjiye, some by Ameena. Ah, great was the acclamation in that room! The news went about and women and girls rushed into the kitchen to congratulate me and Ameena. So, yes, what had I volunteered to do?

It wasn't me. Ameena had volunteered me; she had volunteered herself. Hassan had agreed. Hejjiye had agreed. Ameena's plan was simple. We could exchange the two Kurdish prisoners for our freedom: we hand them over to the Peshmerga forces in the ruins behind us, and they allow our convoy to cross the field and this end of the town, controlled by the Kurds, so that we could join our Daesh folk and Hejjiye's beloved Commander Abu Jalal on the other side. Ingenious, wasn't it?

Not so ingenious. Remember, I was being blessed; Ameena was being blessed. Surely such a simple plan would not have showered us with Hejjiye's blessings, not to mention Allah's mercy by proxy? Think of it. How would it work? Would the Kurds simply allow us to drive away, trusting that we were leaving behind the prisoners, and alive too? Would we hand them the prisoners and trust them to let us drive away afterward? You have no idea of what it is like out there if you think that any side would trust the other even an inch!

But Ameena, the strategist, had an even better plan.

What if a deal was struck with the Kurds, so that they allowed *most* of us to leave? A ceasefire could be arranged. They could even allow vans from the town to come and get us. We would agree to leave behind only three or four men, who could hand the prisoners over, and return in the armoured carrier. As the Kurdish forces were still waiting for their heavy weaponry to catch up with their advance forces, an armoured carrier would leave the men with a good chance of reaching their own lines even if the Kurds reneged on their promise after the prisoners were released.

Sounds good? You are underestimating Ameena. She had done even better than that.

Think of it like this: why should the Kurds trust us to the extent of letting most of us reach safety? What if, after we reached safety, our men shot the Peshmerga women and then used the armoured carrier to fight their way back to Daesh lines? It was possible. The armoured personnel carrier—that was when I learned that it was an advanced and much coveted American M113 APC—could do it. What prevented Hassan from doing so right now was the presence of women and men who could not fit into just one carrier.

The solution, you ask? Two women should remain behind; after the rest of us reached our lines, these two women would escort the Kurdish prisoners to the ruins on the other side, walk back, and pull out with only three or four men waiting in our American M113 APC. The presence of the women would reassure the Kurds that their women would not be harmed. Those two women were to be Ameena and me.

Brilliant, no? Would it have worked? No, I am not sure it would have—because, on its own, Hassan might not have trusted even us. Why should he trust us to return? Hassan was no idiot. What if we switched sides and stayed back? That would not be allowed: given our "trophy of the faith" status in those circles, we could never be lost again to the faithless West. But Ameena had gone one up on that too; her idea, born out of her determination to be a martyr, as I gathered then, had preempted that doubt.

Remember the blessings showered on us? That was be-cause we were not just going to escort Dilnaz and Sera to the ruins; we were going to bear suicide vests, smuggled in with the vans that would be sent to fetch the rest of us. Once we reached the other side, we would blow ourselves up, decimat-ing their numbers and giving the leftover men time to escape in their carrier. Evidently, according to Ameena, it had been my idea, blessings upon my devotion, may I be the mother of … oops, well anyway, blessings, blessings, blessings!

Ah, yes, you see the loophole there. Good for you; you should write a thriller next time! What if we did not blow ourselves up? What if, once we reached the Kurds, we took off our suicide vests and threw them away? You underesti-mate Ameena's strategy. Hassan was to be in control. There would be a remote device in the vests; he could blow us up from inside the orphanage. We did not even have to take the trouble of killing ourselves. He would do it for us.

Brilliant, no? You say *ingenious*? Well, maybe.

***

You are a novelist, and novelists love irony, don't they? That is what Mrs. Chatterji thought. "People who do not understand irony cannot understand fiction," she would tell us, hopping around. I suppose you must have spotted the irony—oh well, one of the many little ironies—in my situation. I had not left England just to avoid getting married, but certainly, at one level, my mother's bid to marry me off had acted as a catalyst. And here I was with Hejjiye—more of a pushy mother than my Ammi could ever be—who had been urging me to get married. So, if Mrs. Chatterji was right, the novelist in you must be wondering: isn't it ironic that I let Ameena's fiction of suicide bombing—it was a fiction about me, for I had no intention of dying like Ameena—stay uncontested because I was now stuck in a place where, sooner or later, I would have to choose between marriage or death? And where, in any case, even marriage might end in death?

If the only way to stay alive was to marry another Hassan, then, I guess, I would do it. But where was even a Hassan around me? We were barred from the men, and there was no Internet any longer! Surrounded by death—and, what was worse, rumours of it, discussion of it, and ceaseless glorification of it in this world and the next—I had become convinced that if there was evidence of divinity in anything on earth, it was in life. Without the miracle of life, there was no God. You might laugh inwardly and think that I was just finding justification for preserving my own miserable little life. Yes, I was, I don't deny it, but this conviction—that life was a gift from Allah and hence priceless, and that only Allah had the right to take life as only He could give it—this conviction that life was worth preserving under any condition, this almost—truly?—religious conviction had grown in me, and it has not diminished since then.

But I will be honest. I won't deny it: I wanted to preserve my life most of all. I had no wish to die, and that too for a cause I no longer believed in—a cause that, perhaps, I had never believed in, for what I had imagined of jihadi life when I was still back in England had been largely a figment of my imagination, born of my desire to live my own faith and my resentment at a culture that, I had felt, did not permit it.

But Ameena had left me with no choice. How could I preserve my miserable little life? Ameena had whispered into my ear, while embracing me in joy, what would happen to me if I tried to back out of martyrdom. I was convinced she would carry out her threat: tell them that I did not want to join her because I did not have true faith. Imagine what it would mean, she had hissed, humiliation … whipping … beheading! And aloud she had proclaimed: "My sister, how blessed am I to have you as my friend!"

I knew they would believe her—their pet suicide bomber that she had become. I was sure of that. Even Umm Layth would not dare speak up for me, given that twist. Ameena had left me with no choice: I could either die, swiftly, with her, or be punished and left to die in pain and suffering. I had never thought I cared so much about my own life. I had never imagined I cared so much for this world—torn, rotten, confusing, unjust though it might be at times. I had never thought I could hate someone so much as I hated Ameena then. But I could not even show my hatred, not fully, not sufficiently for it to afford me any relief.

So I did what Ammi used to do, and at that moment I understood my mother: I took to my copy of the Quran, and read it over and over again. They left me alone. They thought I was preparing for the mission. They thought I was preparing for my death. But what I was thinking of—as my eyes moved unthinkingly over the familiar, now meaningless lines—was Ameena's plan. I kept imagining her walking into Hejjiye's office and laying it all down for her beloved Hassan to grasp, her dark eyes glancing up for his approbation as they used to solicit Alex's admiration once upon a time. I saw it in my mind, as if I, not Hejjiye, had accompanied her. I saw her explain—Hassan was not stupid, but he was no great strategist either, and he must have been suspicious of her. Maybe that is why she needed to suggest that the idea had come from me? I saw her lay it down step by step, simply enough for Hassan to understand and buy her package: broker a ceasefire, allow the bulk of us to be driven out on the condition that the two Peshmerga prisoners would be released. Not all, or the other side would not agree to it. Keep some jihadis to assure the other side, offer her and me as hostages, so to say, and then the master stroke: the bomb vests she and I would bear as we escorted the Peshmerga women over to the other side, so that, finally, Hassan could claim a victory, not a bargain, not a surrender. He would never have agreed to a simple exchange. It would have left his career and reputation in tatters. Ameena would have known that. Hassan would not have agreed to a bargain without that final twist of the bomb vests. In the pages of my Quran, I saw Ameena's eyes light up, as they used to once upon a time, then with puckish humour, now with murderous fanaticism, when Hassan agreed and set about negotiating.

***

No, the firing had not ceased because of the asr prayers.

A ceasefire was in place. The Kurds had agreed to Ameena's brilliant plan—of course, they had no idea how ingenious it was. Not yet.

SUICIDE BOMBER

Do you understand the deal Ameena had worked out? This was it: The ceasefire would continue into the next day. It would continue until our women and children were driven to the other side of the town, behind the frontlines, in exchange for the prisoners. Two women would have to stay and accompany the Kurdish prisoners—a woman for a woman, you might say!—but not more than four jihadi men could stay back. Once the women had been delivered, the two accompanying women would be allowed back and the group would be given half an hour to leave the area. If they stayed longer than half an hour, the building would be bombed. The heavier guns, which were following, would be in place by Friday. There would be no mercy after that, the Peshmerga colonel had warned Hassan and his men.

I am sure Ameena had worked it out, down to the finest detail, with Hejjiye's help. It seemed to be beyond Hassan.

The day diminished. I said my prayers out of habit, not able to think of anything apart from my own imminent death. Just one more night. Just one more night of life! No one else seemed to care. Umm Layth was the only woman who had tried to dissuade Ameena. She did it in public.

She said, during the dinner, which was sparse enough: "Daughter, what you are doing will surely give you a place in the highest heavens, but will you consider this poor, il-literate woman's thoughts, too? This poor old woman does not have your learning, and surely she talks nonsense, being illiterate, but she thinks, and Allah knows that to hide an honest thought in your heart is wrong, for surely Allah sees all and hears all, yes, even what we bear in our hearts, and so, I say to you, daughter, reconsider your glorious resolve, for surely the role of a woman is to give birth, not to throw bombs."

Ameena looked at her and smiled—she never smiled any longer—and for once I glimpsed the Ameena I had known once, the girl with the shadow of hurt in her eyes. Where had that shadow disappeared? In her eyes now there was an angry hardness that seemed to have come to her as a bridal gift from Hassan! But no, having given Umm Layth a slight smile, Ameena put her head down and started eating from our plate again. She did not even bother to reply! This was also Ameena: unbending and resolved, once her mind was made up.

Hejjiye made no such attempt as Umm Layth, who, I could see, had taken some risk in trying to dissuade Ameena, as her convoluted speech indicated. Then, suddenly, it was dark, the sudden night of those parts, so different from what I had grown up with in England, like a curtain had fallen on the sun. We said our last prayers and went to bed in silence. Hardly anyone talked, unless it was to instruct or comfort a child. The silence seemed greater because, unusually, there was no gunfire immediately around us. Despite the unexpected quietness of the night, I could hardly sleep. I lay down, sat up, walked around in our narrow room, said an extra prayer on my bed, and lay down to sleep again. I got up many times, and sat on the edge of the cot, determined to say something to Ameena. But she slept on, soundly, with a peaceful expression on her face, and I realised there was nothing I could say to her. I even contemplated going to Hejjiye—she was sleeping upon the cot in the corridor, outside the cell—and throwing myself on her mercy. But that seemed to be an even less likely option.

I must have fallen asleep, because I woke up to the sound of people moving in the corridor—and a strange peaceful song in my ears. It took me a second to realise that it was the muezzin's call from the Town. We had heard it in the past, but recently the shooting and bombing had drowned it out. Now I could hear it again in the silent dawn. I performed my ablutions and said the dawn prayer, simply out of habit.

***

Two white flags appeared on the Peshmerga side, as agreed. Hassan's men put up a white flag too. Nothing else happened for the next two hours. We shared out our last ration of dry bread and biscuits. Coffee had run out, but there was some tea. For once none of the women argued about how to brew the tea. The silence grew with the sunshine. For the first time in two or three days, I heard the cry of birds—oh well, it was a crow, but even a crow's croaking sounded wonderful. There still was life. There were birds and breeze. There were clouds in the blue sky. And we could look at them for a moment, hear them again. You have no idea how beautiful the world looks and sounds in the hours after a battle stops!

A bit before noon, two covered trucks drove into the courtyard. They had been sent, with only a driver in each, from the town by our people. One of them must have smuggled in the suicide vests that formed the secret, infernal part of Ameena's plan. Hassan's armoured carrier also pulled up and blocked the entrance to the courtyard, as the gate was left ajar.

When both sides were certain that they would not be deceived, Hassan issued instructions to his men and, stealthily, one by one, they started sneaking back from their posts or bunkers elsewhere. Some were injured; one had to be carried in a litter. Mostly, they stayed in the open courtyard, clustering around the trucks and the armoured carrier. One or two joined Hassan and his two men in the classroom. In the meanwhile, the women ran around in the curtained corridor of our wing, bundling up their meagre possessions again, making sure their children stayed in sight. Hejjiye supervised this part of it. The two Kurdish prisoners remained in their cell, their hands chained together as a special precaution. I could hear them moving. Ameena sat on the cot outside their cell. She read from a small Quran, or so it appeared to me. As the cell was at the other end of the corridor, and all the windows were boarded up, she had a candle to read by. It lighted up the end of the corridor, making it shine like some mysterious cave.

Umm Layth came to bless me and went down the corridor to bless Ameena. I could see them, hear the old woman murmur her tribal blessings indistinctly. I noticed that Ameena didn't acknowledge the old woman's blessings. She kept her head bowed over the book, reading in the candlelight. But she gave Hejjiye a far warmer farewell. Hejjiye had supervised the embarkation of the women and the children. Then, at the last moment, with the serene confidence that she always oozed, Hejjiye went up to Ameena and handed her the ring of keys—to the hand-cuffs and the padlocks on the prisoners' cell—which had been in her smart Gucci bag until then. Hejjiye also gave Ameena a rosary of blue beads. "Take this to Allah with you, O Blessed One," she said. Ameena embraced Hejjiye with great fervour. Hejjiye had said a few words of appreciation to me too. I am glad she did not give me a gift, as it would have made me break down—from the sheer effort to refrain from flinging her beads in her face! Instead, she had a homily or two for me. I hardly heard them: How does that poem go, the one we read in school?... at my back, I could hear death's winged chariot hurrying near. That was all the sound I could hear. Believe me. It drowned out the murmur of Hejjiye's words.

But I still recall that there was no sign of doubt in Hejjiye's broad, handsome face as she left; no realisation that she had just given a trinket to someone who was going to die for her sake, while she herself, ever pious, always good in her own eyes, was being driven to safety. It struck me that people like Hejjiye are always driven to safety—and in all cultures. At that moment, I finally saw Hejjiye as I would always remember her, as I recall her now: she was a person who would be at home, and in control and totally satisfied with herself, anywhere. She could have been a politician in Europe, justifying racist immigration laws in the most humane terms; she could have been a corporate head in New York or a banker in Tokyo. Whatever set of rules she found around herself, she would employ to empower herself, not even able to see the monstrous shadows thrown by her goodness. It was only a fluke, I felt, that Hejjiye had been born in circles where the route to power lay through the strictures of Islam. People like her always manage to be driven to safety while someone else dies for their causes.

And yet—for I have come to live with doubt, yes, to welcome doubt as a condition of life and faith—I sometimes wonder if, at the same time, Hejjiye was not responsible for keeping dozens of women, children, orphans alive, for creating an oasis for their preservation in the deserts of violence that surrounded them?

It was soon after the noon prayers that Hejjiye, Umm Layth, the other women, and the children left. They crowded into one of the covered trucks, and two jihadis got into the driver's section. The injured men were helped or carried into the other covered truck. Hardly any wishes were exchanged. The armoured carrier was backed away to enable the lorries to leave. They drove out and waited, on the street next to the guardhouses, their engines running, white flags flying from them. Hassan's cargo van entered the courtyard now. I had forgotten all about its existence; its windows were shattered. The machine gun on our roof was taken down and mounted on the van again.

Then, after some iPhone and wireless messages, Hejjiye's convoy left in a cloud of smoke and dust. No, we did not say goodbye in the courtyard. There were men there. I was relieved to be left in the building, observing but not observed, with Ameena.

The van led. We saw them take a turn, pass behind a mound of earth with clumps of bushes on it, and then proceed across the stretch of plain agricultural fields—now barren— that lay between us and the Town. The unusual silence grew. Now there were just three men left, and Hassan. And us, the women: the two Kurdish women soldiers, still in chains, Ameena, me. The courtyard was empty, too, apart from the sole M113 APC, which was being driven back into it.

With the convoy out of sight, Hassan and his man closed the heavy gate. They walked back to the building. Ameena and I retired to our curtained section. Hassan's man went into the main office to rejoin his comrades keeping a lookout from its windows, but Hassan turned and walked toward our corridor. I could see him as a shadow across the reed curtain: a broad man carrying an M4 rifle, his trademark black dagger tucked into his belt. He did not cross over into our area.

He stopped there and shouted: "It is time, women!" He spoke Arabic, not English; I suspected he did not wish to be reminded of our origins.

Ameena seemed to jerk up at the sound of his voice, as if a volt of electricity had passed through her. Then she collected herself and said, dully, "I am here, my husband. I am ready to do your bidding and God's."

"Is your friend ready too?"

"Yes, she is, Allah be praised.'

"No, I am not," I felt like shouting out. But what was the use? What good would it do? I had no chance, and I had lain awake most of the night pondering over the matter. What could I do? It seemed to me that there was just one option—I had to tell the Kurdish women that Ameena and I were wearing bomb vests. I had to tell them that we were not just escorting them to the Peshmerga side as security, but that having reached their side, we would detonate ourselves, killing them and as many of their men as we could. Perhaps then we could make a run for it—but only after Hassan and his men allowed us to start walking across the field. They might shoot us, they might miss. Ameena would detonate her vest, I was certain. But I wouldn't; I would rip it off, throw it as far as I could and try to run to safety. There was a chance we would make it, if we managed to walk some distance away from Hassan and the orphanage building before we made a break for it. That was my plan. What I did not know was if the Kurdish women would understand me quickly enough, or even if I would have the time to say all this to them in the couple of minutes that I would have between the time we started walking away from Hassan and his men and the time we could run for cover? Would I be able to get rid of my vest before Hassan realised and used his remote detonator? Ameena would be there too, walking with us. What would that mean? Would she say something to confuse the women? And if the women did not understand me or believe me, surely, I would have no chance but to run on my own—and if I did so, without the Kurdish women shouting to their side not to open fire, I would be gunned down from both sides!

I had tried to reach the cell of the Kurdish women when they were alone, but Ameena must have been afraid of something like that: she had made sure that there was a watch over them all the time. Always her or Hejjiye, since the moment her blessed plan had been revealed to us. Long entrusted with the care of the Kurdish women, after she sidled her way into Hejjiye's favours and relieved me of that task, I knew that Ameena appeared to get along well with the two Kurdish women, who had no idea of the gory fate she had planned for them. It made me hate her even more.

You are a writer; you think you know about matters such as love and hate, or you would not dare write of them. But, believe me, you have no idea what real hate is. You cannot even begin to imagine how much I hated Ameena. It was like a bottomless pit in my heart; you would not believe, looking at me today, that someone like me could be capable of such implacable hatred, and that, for a woman who was once her best friend!

***

Ameena had been careful and devious. She had planned this out to the last detail, whatever her reason: perverted faith or love, sheer vainglory, or just the last act of a woman who could not concede, to the world and herself, that most of her acts had been misguided. You know how it happens when sometimes one starts arguing, knowing well that one is in the wrong, and this knowledge just makes one get more vicious and unbending in argument? I wondered if all of Ameena's much-vaunted piety and faith were not just an extreme version of that tendency in human beings. She knew she was wrong, and because of that, because she would not concede it to herself, she was going to go even further in her argument.

But then, something happened that I was not prepared for. I almost felt like laughing. I thought that, finally, Allah—the true Allah, not Ameena's and Hassan's Allah—had come to my rescue. Because, as Ameena spoke to her husband across the reed partition, I realised that her well-wrought plan contained a flaw—from her and Hassan's orthodox perspective. Of course, Hassan had not seen the flaw yet. But Ameena had, and it was she who mentioned it to Hassan.

They spoke in whispers about it, across the reed screen, as they obviously did not want the Kurdish prisoners to overhear them. But I was standing near Ameena. I overheard most of it. And, in any case, they had no reason to hide it from me: this one flaw in Ameena's ingenious plan, something that they had not detected until then.

***

Can you spot the flaw? No? Oh well, you never lived in that world.

You see, Ameena was Hassan's wife, and she could easily unveil in front of him, so that he could rig her up with the bomb vest. But what about me? There was no man there—no brother, no husband, no father—who could approach, let alone touch me, unveiled. And obviously, our bomb vests had to be hidden under our clothes, or the Kurdish women would realise what we were up to.

"Jamilla, here, is such a devout woman. And it would be wrong, even for a woman less devout than Jamilla," Ameena told Hassan.

I thought it was an indication of Ameena's demented fanaticism that she assumed that such a small thing could be an issue for me: she was willing to consider such a petty matter while at the same time volunteering me for a gory death; she wanted to preserve my modesty while blowing my body to bits! I could have laughed out aloud in any other circumstance.

But this was not a major problem in Ameena's view. She had been quick in sorting it out. She would accompany Hassan to a room, where he could install a bomb vest on her and teach her how to install the other one on me. Then, she would return and do so in a room of our women's wing and both of us, fully veiled, could then escort the Kurdish prisoners as planned. Elementary. God is great!

Yes, I thought, God was great: because this would give me the few minutes I needed to explain the conspiracy to Dilnaz and Sera. We would then, perhaps, have a chance to run for it when we approached the Peshmerga section.

Ah, I see you pause: why, you are wondering, did Hassan need to teach us how to blow ourselves up, when he could do it for us, thank you so much? No, it was not just a tactical matter. Perhaps it was that, too. Perhaps. He must have realised that we could do greater damage if we chose the moment to detonate our vests; we would be among the Kurds, and he would be at a distance, unable to have a clear view. But, no, you cannot understand people like Hassan if you attribute just tactical or practical motives to their actions. A person like Hassan believes in choice of a sort as much as any free-market capitalist does, and the choice is just as limited. Surprised? No, it is true; I am convinced of it. Only, the choice in the case of people like Hassan is death: Hassan would never deny a fellow Muslim the choice of death for the glory of his Allah.

That is what Islam was for him, a hankering after death, from a choice of Muslims, *true* Muslims, for what greater evidence of submission to the will of Allah can there be but voluntary death, and death imposed on everyone else, including *false* Muslims; that is, all Muslims who would not choose death. Voluntary death by a Muslim satisfied a deeper level of blood-lust in Hassan—and I am certain it also justified, in his mind, the violence he inflicted on others, on non-Muslims and *false* Muslims. No, Hassan would blow us up only if we failed to do so ourselves.

***

"Allow me to put on my veil and I will come with you,

my husband," I heard Ameena say in her laboured, stilted, copybook Arabic. It was a needless statement, made just to stress her piety. Like all the women, since our noon prayers, she already had her veil on. She just needed to draw her visage sheet in place. She did so.

Then she turned to me and said, in the semidark, loudly and slowly enough for Hassan to be able to overhear: "A'm happy yer met me that day and cured me of smoking. These holy beads A give to yer as thanks for showing me the right path. Wear 'em 'round yer neck."

She put something in my hand and walked briskly out of the section. As I heard Hassan and her walk away, I looked at what I held. It was the rosary of blue beads given to Ameena by Hejjiye. I might have flung them away, but entangled in them were also the keys to the cell of the Kurdish women and to their chains.

I could not believe my eyes. Did she trust me so much in what she thought were our last moments? Had she really fooled herself to such an extent that she believed that I shared her fanaticism, too? Or had she just made a mistake, and handed me the keys because they were entangled in the prayer beads?

***

I did not spend too much time thinking about her reasons. As soon as Hassan and Ameena had walked away, I rushed in the opposite direction down the corridor. The candle was still illuminating that end. I fumbled to open the cell door, indicating to the women to be silent. They looked happy to see me. Then, slowly, so as not to make a noise, I unlocked their chains and handcuffs.

All this must have taken a few minutes. I was breathless, so excited that my hands were shaking; I started stuttering when I tried to tell them of Ameena's plans. But Dilnaz put a finger to her lips. Hush, she said. Hush.

I thought Hassan had come back. But there was no one in the corridor.

I turned back to Sera and Dilnaz, trying to calm myself in order to describe the conspiracy with some lucidity. Dilnaz said something to Sera, who interpreted as she used to all those weeks ago.

"We know," said Sera. "She says, stay calm, we know. She says your friend is a brave woman."

Dilnaz shook her head and added in her limited English, "Good woman."

***

I did not know what to say. Were the two women stark raving mad? How could they know? Why should Ameena have told them? Or Hejjiye? What did they mean by saying that my friend was a good woman? Ameena, that rabid suicide bomber?

I was going to say something more, but Dilnaz and Sera guided me firmly into one of the rooms. I was too bewildered to resist. Softly they closed the door, without bolting it. Dilnaz raised a hand for silence—I guess I was still trying to babble my explanations and questions—and seemed to listen. A minute or two later, there was an unearthly shriek—a woman's shriek. It came from the men's section. It sounded like a name to me, a name I knew.

As if Dilnaz and Sera had been waiting for this cue, they pushed me down to the floor, throwing themselves on top of me. I think realisation must have begun to dawn on me then, and at that very moment there was the loudest explosion I have ever heard. It was like the world had come to an end. Waves of sound passed through us, and the blast of a wind that seemed to penetrate the thick walls and roofs. The building shook. Chunks of plaster fell on us. I screamed. I think I must have screamed. I couldn't hear myself. Dilnaz kept holding me down. She kept holding me down for at least a couple of minutes more as I struggled—I did not really know why—to get out of her grip. Then the building seemed to shudder and sigh like a sad old man, and everything grew eerily quiet. Dilnaz finally let me go. I crawled on all fours. Our door was hanging from a hinge. Sera came and put her arms around me. She was bleeding from a slight cut under her hairline, blood mixing with tears and dripping down her cheek. I realised I was weeping helplessly; my body was racked with sobs, which came in waves, like the tide in the ocean, sweeping up from some immense depth of grief that I could not even see.

I was only now beginning to understand what Ameena had done. I found that I was still holding that rosary of blue beads that Hejjiye had given her, and she had given me. Here it is. See. This is all I have of the person who was my best friend and whom I once hated more than I thought I could hate anyone, more than I thought it was human to hate. And it does not even belong to her. It belongs to a woman who could never have understood someone like Ameena. I wonder what Mrs. Chatterji would have made of the irony of it?

***

Dilnaz helped me patch together the story: Ameena had told Dilnaz of her plan to enable them to escape and to enable me to have a life again. Dilnaz had discussed it with her to the extent it was possible to talk about such matters without being overheard. Sera had translated, as she did for me, and English was almost a code, but one could not be certain. And Hejjiye, fluent in English, had been in the building. Yet, Dilnaz had tried to dissuade Ameena. She did not want to gain her own freedom in that manner; now, she said, she will be indebted to Ameena to the last breath of her life. But Ameena had been persuasive: three lives, one death, she had argued. She had been adamant.

"She felt you were caught in this place because of her," Dilnaz told me. "She felt there was no one who could broker for your release and the Daesh would not let either you or her go on your own. She felt she had landed you in a horrible mess."

"She hadn't," I replied. "It was I who ... But why didn't she tell me?"

Dilnaz smiled: "Would you have gone along with it? Would you have allowed her to die for you?"

Would I have? I don't know. I do recall that I had wanted to live, I had wanted desperately to live, and I had hated Ameena for volunteering me and herself as suicide bombers.

So, yes, once again I patched together her story. I can imagine her last moments. I can imagine Hassan putting the vest on her in some room, or perhaps even a curtained corner of Hejjiye's office, which they were using as their headquarters. I can see him explaining to her how to put a vest on me, how to detonate the vests. I can see her pulling her niqab back on and following Hassan out of the partitioned section—or room, if it was a separate room—and back to the main office, from where the other three men were keeping an eye on the Kurdish positions in the ruins. There, a woman dressed entirely in black, with only her eyes showing, facing those four armed men, one of them her husband, the husband she had left a civilisation for, there, with the huge black Daesh flag on one wall, this ordinary-looking woman with the shadow of a hurt in her eyes, there she had shrieked out that strange name as a signal for us to take cover—and she had blown herself and the four men to smithereens.

Yes, I patched together her story—but can I truly understand her? Can anyone? I like to remember her now as she said I had first met her, a small lonely girl puffing away fiercely at a cigarette behind the slide in a damp, grey, littered school playground; a waif, a wick.

**

It took us a few days to leave the region and get in touch with the higher-ups. But I had not been wrong about Dilnaz. She was not just any ordinary soldier. She was an officer, and a high office-holder of the PKK. After the Peshmerga forces rescued us from the rubble, she took me under her wing. She said she had promised Ameena. I could live with her as her own daughter, she said. No one would look for me among them; no one would harass me. The media had already reported my death along with Ameena's—I don't know how, but it had been in the newspapers in England too. "British Jihadis Die in Skirmish." "Western Casualties Fighting for ISIS." "Drone Kills Jihadi Janes." Google up the headlines; you will find them. There was even a photo of a prayer meeting held at our old mosque for us.

But I had no wish to stay in that part of the world anymore. I had seen too much violence; I had heard too much religion. And I could never share the conviction of Dilnaz, who was, after all, a fighter, a believer in the cause of free Kurdistan, and hence someone who made sense of Ameena's death in ways that were now partly hollow to me: sacrifice, historical justice, national freedom.

Dilnaz also asked me if I would like to go back home. But, no, I could not. It was not that I would be faced with policemen and legal matters, those I could take, those I might even have welcomed. But I did not want to bring more trouble into my mother's life: she must have cried over me, she must have said the prayers for the dead by now. Could I thrust her back into her loss again, and compound it with legal hassles and worries? What could I bring to her but greater worries, maybe even persecution? Could I even spend time with her in her last years? Surely I would be jailed, at least for a few years, on my return. And there was another mother I could not face: I could not face Ameena's parents. Her mother, what could I say to Aunty? What could I ever say to her? What about my brother or Ali, you ask. Yes, what about them? These were, these are the people I would have to petition for help if I returned and went through the process of the law. Cases, lawyers, media, fees. I did not want their help. I did not even want to have to explain to them: all those believers who would never do what Hassan did or Hejjiye enabled, but who would insist on a similarly narrow interpretation of religion and God. I could not hold them responsible for the madness of militant Islamism, as so much of the Western media conveniently does, but I could not absolve them entirely either! Above all, strange as this may sound, I could not go back to them and still retain my own faith. If I went back to their unquestioning Islam, I would have to abandon my Allah of the endless doubts!

I had to go somewhere else.

Dilnaz was true to her word. She arranged for false identity papers, a fake passport. She arranged for an airplane ticket. She wanted to go to Istanbul to put me on a plane herself, but she was dissuaded by her friends; there was a chance the Turkish authorities would arrest her as a Kurdish rebel. Instead, she saw me off from the bus stop and, at the last moment, put to me the question that must have been worrying her.

"Your friend," she said, "Your great friend, the martyr Ameena, may Allah rest her in peace, why did she shout out 'Sabah' as a warning for us to take cover? Why 'Sabah'?"

So it was true. I had not imagined it: the strange, unexpected name I thought I had heard just before the explosion … Ameena's last word had been that cry, almost unhuman, that name, the long never-ending Sabaaaa …which I still hear on some nights, and thrash about in bed, pinioned and helpless and wanting to run and help her, unable, unable, unable forever, unable even to return to her that last loving caress, when she had patted my hair in place, unable for all eternity, unless, of course, I hope you understand, there is a merciful God, a loving Allah.

What could I tell Dilnaz?

I lied.

"Sabah was her son," I replied.

"What happened to him?" Dilnaz asked me, her face filling with sorrow and concern.

"He died. He died a long time ago."

***

It is almost dark now. See, see the birds flying in to roost in that milkwood tree. Do you know that most of the masks they make here are made of the wood of that tree? Do you suppose that is why it is called "milkwood"? Because it can be poured into any shape, like milk?

Anyway, ignore my tears; they will dry. I won't pretend it is a gust from the window. It is getting late; I should be in my room by now. Batala will be restless, clawing at the door. Yes, what else? I have a cat now. Nothing fancy, just a striped kitten I picked up from the street. I called it Batala; I am not very original, am I? There, that's better; dry eyes.

I have to go; I have come to the end of my story. See, when Dilnaz and her companions asked me where I wished to go, I said, Indonesia. Why Indonesia? Perhaps because it seemed farthest away from everything I had known until then.

Why, you still ask me.

Well, why not? Ameena's death had been reported—killed in an explosion, it was said—and I was presumed dead with her. There was no need to change that story. What could I go back and say to Ammi? What could I say to Aunty? Would even James, who always tried to understand me in school, be able to understand me now? To defend my faith against accusations from this side or that, to be unable to speak from my bewildered heart even to my own family and friends—why return to such a past? I wanted a place where I had no history, and where I could be with my beliefs without people who proscribed or prescribed.

But that is why I came to you. That is why I had to speak to you. I could not make up my mind about what

I thought of your statement last night during your reading—that people like me ought not to be allowed back to any democratic, yes, let's say it, any civilised place. No, I would not want to go back to England. I cannot imagine going back, now or ever. But what about Ameena, had she lived? What would she have wished, if she'd had a choice?

I don't know. Do you?

ACKNOWLEDGEMENTS

Isabelle Petiot, Claire Chambers (and her family), Gulzar, Neel Mukerjee, Bina Shah, Jim Hicks, Liz Jensen, Sharmilla Beezmohun, Beatrice Hitchman, Seb Doubinsky, Annette Lindegaard, Ellen Dengel-Janic, Conrad Nelson of Northern Lights, Michel Moushabeck, Mitch Albert, Meru Gokhale, Anushree Kaushal, Rachita Raj, Kirsten Syppli Hansen, Jessica Woollard, and my agents, Mita Kapur and Matt Bialer

READER'S GUIDE

Prepared by Anna Botta; Maryam Fatima; Asha Nadkarni

I. Issues of Narration

The novel's main story is told by Jamilla, one of two protagonists, to a male writer entrusted with the task of writing up both her story and the story of her best friend Ameena. Readers are constantly reminded of the differences between the setting and time in which Jamilla tells this story and the locations and times of the story she tells.

How do the multiple layers of mediation and narration complicate the story and shape our relationship to the two protagonists? Is the story changed by being filtered through Jamilla and the writer who listens to her story?

What role does Wendy Cope's poem "Reading Scheme" play in alerting us to the role of irony, and to the difference between fact and fiction? What does Jamilla's reading of the poem tell us about her as a narrator? Given that "Reading Scheme" is also the title of the novel's opening chapter, could Tabish Khair be suggesting indirectly how his novel, and, more generally, literature ought to be read?

Jamilla tells her story to a male author who, as we can discern from some of her comments to him, may potentially be hostile to her views. She repeats, for instance, a statement that the author made at a public reading she attended:

"that people like [her] ought not to be allowed back to any democratic, yes, let's say it, any civilised place" (220). Is Jamilla trying to justify her position to the narrator—and thus to the reader as well? Is her story an act of atonement, motivated by guilt? How does she try to get him (and us) on her side?

How much do we trust that this is Ameena's story? Does Jamilla try to absolve herself by blaming Ameena (think, for example, about how Jamilla often compares herself to her passive mother)?

How much does the fictional writer portrayed in the novel have in common with the author, Tabish Khair—the writer of novels such as *How to Fight Islamist Terror from the Missionary Position* (Interlink Books, 2014) and critical essays such as those in *The New Xenophobia* (Oxford University Press, 2016)?

II. Issues of Translation

Much of the novel is engaged in acts of translation, but it also faces the limits of translatability. Jamilla attempts to translate her experience (culture, language, religion) to a man who is then supposed to translate it to us. Think about the ways in which the novel performs these different levels of translation successfully and also where it works less well.

The epigraph—an excerpt from Tony Harrison's poem "v."—presents us with a series of black and white oppositions, what the poet calls "the versuses of life." What does the epigraph tell us about translation? How does the novel introduce forms of multiplicity and differences which undermine the absolute character of such "either/or" dichotomies?

Although the novel presents us with characters, such as Hassan and Hejjiye, who understand the world in terms of absolutes, it also shows us that there are no true spaces of purity (think, for instance, of Hejjiye's Gucci handbag collection). What then is the novel saying about the idea of purity, particularly in reference to religion? Comment on the passage:

> Why did Allah have to create Shaitan, God have to create Satan? Why create evil? … [W]hy test humanity if you are all-powerful and purely good?… The answer—don't laugh at me—that I have now is this: evil is a precondition to goodness. Goodness reveals itself only in its capacity to tolerate the pettiness and dullness of evil (118)

III. The Issue of Irony

Comment on the following passage:

> You are a novelist, and novelists love irony, don't they? That is what Mrs. Chatterji thought. "People who do not understand irony cannot understand fiction," she would tell us, hopping around. I suppose you must have spotted the irony—oh well, one of the many little ironies—in my situation. I had not left England just to avoid getting married, but certainly, at one level, my mother's bid to marry me off had acted as a catalyst. And here I was with Hejjiye—more of a pushy mother than my Ammi could ever be—who had been urging me to get married. (196)

IV. Communities and Conflicts

In which ways does the novel establish connections and build communities between East and West, across religious divisions, or between country folk and city people? How does it contribute in showing the complexity of the ethnic and religious landscape of the Middle East?

V. Gender

Tabish Khair's previous novel, How to Fight Islamist Terror from the Missionary Position *(Interlink Books, 2014) looked at Islamization in Europe from a male-centered perspective— its three main characters are all men.* Just Another Jihadi Jane, *in contrast, presents female perspectives on the same theme.*

What does the novel say about the construction of femininity and masculinity in the different cultural contexts it portrays?

How does the novel highlight how difficult it is to be observant in the West—especially for a woman? Comment on the intersections of gender and religion brought up by Jamilla in the following passage:

> [T]rust me, no man, no Muslim man, no matter how believing, how faithful, how orthodox, has to face a third of the difficulties that orthodox Muslim women encounter in the West.... You opt out of the glitter of the West, because of your belief. It takes strength to do so. More strength than Muslim men realise: I wonder if imams would insist on the hijab as much as they do, if they had to put it on themselves and cope with the consequences in ordinary life. It takes strength and character. (77–8)

Part of the work done by this novel is found in its exploration of the gendered dimensions of Islamist radicalization—and it does so against the usual depiction of terrorists as male. Instead Khair's novel shows how Muslim men are often moved by self-serving reasons to look favorably on their daughters' Islamization. See, for example, the passage that criticizes Ameena's father, noting his "male assumption that his child, being a young woman, would be safer with Islam than with the West … Or was it the hypocritical love of a father who considered the freedoms that he allowed himself, and might have allowed a son, to be unsuitable or dangerous for his daughter?" (43).

An attentive reader will find many sorts of unlikely sisterhoods throughout the novel. What are we meant to think about them? For instance, what does a peasant woman such as Umm Layth have in common with a city girl like Ameena?

VI. Technology and Media

Could technology itself be thought of as a character in the novel? In some regards, the internet is important for creating community, but just how real is that community?

Comment on the following passage:

> Ameena and I … [erased] the differences that existed with the brush of a hypothetical Islam, an imagined community … But what, I wonder now, did we really have in common with the Somalian girl who refused to read anything but the Quran, the Algerian girl whose Islamism was driven by colonial memories of French atrocities instead of any firm religious belief, the Palestinian woman who had

given up on moderate politics because she was convinced that Israeli and American politicians were lying about the two-state solution, or, for that matter, green-eyed Michelle, a stunning nineteen-year-old brunette from a Parisian suburb, a self-confessed "film buff" who had converted to Islam after an online romance with a jihadi she had not even met ... (53-4)

What does technology enable and what does it preclude? Comment on the disparity between tech-savvy ISIS and the deprivation from technology experienced in war zones or Khair's orphanage. What are the consequences of such a disparity?

Think about the novel's portrayal of media. Where do the media stand in relation to what's true and what's false? What can the novel teach us about how to read the media (or even about how to read the novel itself)?

How do traditional forms of media as well as new social media go about creating different personae? For instance, in Hejjiye's case, do you ever get anything behind the performance? What are we meant to make of the comparison on page 134 of ISIS to a catwalk? Do you find this heretical? Clearly what Hejjiye is doing is much more serious than a catwalk. Is this an appropriate comparison?

VII. Fact or Fiction?

How many of the events portrayed in the novel are real? How about the "Jihadi Jane" article mentioned on page 216, "Drone Kills Jihadi Janes"? What does the writer tell us about the relation between believable stories and historical facts?

VIII. Titling the Novel: *Jihadi Jane* or *Just Another Jihadi Jane*?

Given what we know of the struggle of the two friends in ISIS-occupied territory (and of Ameena's sacrifice at the end), does the title do justice to the complexity of their story? Are these two characters just more "Jihadi Janes"? How does the title draw our attention to the ways in which Western media reduces and erases the subjectivity of Muslim women?

IX. Social, Political, and Cultural Spaces

Think about the space of the orphanage and the space of the school in England. Are they different or similar? Both are figured as forms of imprisonment, yet in different ways. Should they be seen as spaces of salvation or spaces of entrapment?

In the novel there are many spaces segregated in terms of gender (think, for instance, of the space of the orphanage). What do such spaces establish for the girls? Why and how is this important?

X. Questions of Blame, of Guilt, of Tolerance

How does the novel deal with the politics of blame? Comment on the following passage: "I could not hold them [believers like Hassan or Hejjiye] responsible for the madness of militant Islamism, as so much of the Western media conveniently does, but I could not absolve them entirely either" (217).

Where does the novel stand against the scriptural injunction not to kill? What does Ameena's final act mean? What does religion say about the function of sacrifice?

XI. Intertextuality

What is Mrs. Chatterji's role in the novel? Is she an important figure?

The controversy over Salman Rushdie's *Satanic Verses* figures in the end of the novel. Why? How does the inclusion of this historical parallel introduce irony?

See the quote from James on page 178: "Once yer start burning books, yer end up burning the entire world, every damn human being in it!" What is the novel's take on this pronouncement?

XII. Islam and the Critique of the West

The novel shows us many different forms of Islam. What are we to make of these diverse communities?

How does the book describe Islam's relationship with the West, even as it challenges monolithic notions of both "Islam" and the "West?" On page 30, Jamilla talks about the convergence between Islam's critique of the West and the leftist perspective. The issues raised by Jamilla here—the arms industry, Guantanamo Bay, lack of international democracy, the inability of the West to hold Israel responsible for human rights violations, the role of oil money in the conflicts of the Middle East—all seem to be reasonable criticisms, levied by many people who aren't necessarily Islamists. How is it different when such criticisms are mobilized by an organization like ISIS?

How do we read Jamilla's move to Indonesia? The story of the novel progresses from England, which is hostile to Islam, to Syria, which is supposedly safe, and ends in Indonesia—a space of moderate Islam (and also a space of exile). What are we meant to make of Jamilla's refusal to disavow her faith, or of her choice to reinterpret her religion in terms of doubt?

XIII. A Final Question

Jamilla ends her narrative with a question addressed to the writer and, indirectly, to us: "No, I would not want to go back to England. I cannot imagine going back, now or ever. But what about Ameena, had she lived? What would she have wished, if she'd had a choice? I don't know, Do you?" (220). Can you venture an answer, given what you know of Ameena?